A Witness for the Demon

By Kevin Wollenweber

"A Witness for the Demon," by Kevin Wollenweber. ISBN 978-1-63868-050-5 (softcover).

Published 2022 by Virtualbookworm.com Publishing Inc., P.O. Box 9949, College Station, TX 77842, US. ©2022, Kevin Wollenweber. All rights reserved. No part of this publication may be reproduced, stored in a retrieval system, or transmitted in any form or by any means, electronic, mechanical, recording or otherwise, without the prior written permission of Kevin Wollenweber.

Chapter 1:
Demetri, the Demon

As HE SAT ON THE BOAT DOCK listening to the water flap against the shoreline. For a brief moment, Demetri felt somewhat mortal. The crickets chirped in what seemed like an orchestrated symphony with the water of the lake keeping time. He wished for a moment he was mortal, but he understood that he never had been, so how could he really know what it was like. A single light flickered above him from an overhang rafter on the dock that began to illuminate the darkening sky.

He recalled sitting on this dock before, but he really could not place when it was. Regardless, it was much older now and the wood had begun to rot. It was rough with an abundance of splinters. Time had taken its toll on this dock, but not on him. He was ageless, handsome, and desirable to all he chose, and he had never been denied.

After more than three thousand years, Demetri thought he should have been challenged by a *host* that might have defeated him. He was a clever angel and endowed with a special gift — to be able to choose a host wisely. What a delightful gift he was provided with from his master, and he used it well.

Still, he wished he could feel hot or cold. Smell the summer smells that permeated the air. Feel the wetness of the water and take a drink of it to quench his thirst, though his thirst was not mortal. Demetri stood up on the dock and glanced around him. All six foot two by human standards with long blonde glowing hair that was braided down the center of his back. He had the power to change the length of his hair and appearance but preferred not to. His physique was like a Viking, muscular, strong, and desirable. The brown skin he adorned mimicked a mortal that would live in a tropical region. Perhaps a surf bum by profession.

Demetri was not a surf bum, but he practiced a much older profession. His talents were honed in his master's image — the talent to *torment*.

The only escape for a fallen angel to not experience an eternity of torment, was to inhabit a host that would absorb it for him. He was a master at administering torment, and he had delivered those tormented souls back to his master. Due to his proficiency in conducting the desires of his master, Demetri had gained favor in his sight. Because of this, he was allowed moments, like now, to sit on a boat dock, on a lake near the coast of Oregon, and wonder what it might be like to be mortal. No torment or pain, no gnashing of teeth, just a quick moment to be deceived into believing what it was like to be human.

Demetri's existence had not always been like today. He still had vivid memories of the day he, and his master, had been cast out of their home. Everything they had known was gone. If it hadn't been for the strength and cunning of his master, his promises for retribution, and the provision in the knowledge that his master was the true god of the universe, Demetri could not imagine how difficult it could have been. His master had promised it was only a matter of time before everything would be made right. He believed him, yet it had been over three thousand years. He dared not challenge his master's word or he would suffer the same pain and torment that those many souls he had indwelled.

In his former home he adored the Angel Gabriel. He looked up to Gabriel and desired to be around him. Even today, he imagines himself to be more like Gabriel than like his master. He believes, today, he would be as powerful as Gabriel if he hadn't made the choice to follow his master. In what might seem like a poor decision to follow Lucifer, Demetri understood his reward for loyalty will be worth it. Still, he wondered when Gabriel visits *this* kingdom, can he feel the water on his feet?

As Demetri stood and surveyed the surrounding landscape of the shores of the lake, he was pleased to see a light illuminating the darkened shoreline of the lake about two hundred yards up from him. He smiled because that meant *souls* had arrived. With this campfire ablaze there would be mortals. Mortals that had not yet made the choice to follow Gabriel's God, and he could show them the way to *his* god.

There was no reason to walk like a human to the fire. Demons could move in a different dimension, just like the Angels of Christ. Just like Gabriel. Demetri knew he could reveal himself to humans if he so desired, but he felt there were so many more effective ways. It was time for him to go to work as he viewed the mortals gathering around the campfire and settling in for their lake party. He recognized his old allies of beer, wine, and various distilled liquors. The one thing that living for three thousand years had taught him, is that there were so many helpers now.

In the eighteenth and nineteenth centuries, Demetri would have to do all the work himself. This would usually involve getting into the mind of his host and say things that would make them believe they were going crazy. Back then there was not much help available for *crazy,* and Demetri took great pleasure in that experience. Now, with all the alcoholic beverages and drugs available, possessing a soul had become a bit mundane. They did all the work for him. As he surveyed the choices before him, his eye caught one young woman sharing a bottle of vodka and passing it on to her other campfire companions. She caught Demetri's attention because she reminded him of another young woman who had *entertained* him in 1920. This girl had all the same features, and although Angels like him could not have physical relations with mortals, he became fond of her. Demetri admired her strong will, and beauty, just like that of his master. For those reasons he chose that woman in 1920, and it could be the reason this girl caught his demon eye now.

This campfire girl would toss back her straight blonde hair, and then produce a smile that was brighter than the fire. She had pale blue eyes that were almost alabaster in color. If it hadn't been for the slightest blue tint in her eyes, he might have thought she was a human without sight. This girl was anything but blind. He wondered why he was so entranced by this human. Perhaps he was still affected by his time spent at the boat dock allowing thoughts of those mortal pleasures to invade his demon mind. Demetri should have been ashamed that he battled with thoughts and desires of the flesh. Then it occurred to him that these were the same feelings he had for the woman in 1920.

He delivered her soul in 1920 to his master by driving her mad and wasn't quite sure if he had ever truly gotten over her. He certainly hadn't forgotten her. Tonight, with this girl, he must be careful as he toys with her thoughts and manipulates her spirit. He did not want to fall into the same trap. A friend came over to Demetri's newest target and bent down to whisper something into her ear. He could make out that this girl was named Cindy.

He rejoiced in glee, "What a delightful name."

As he pondered just how excited he was to indwell this girl, the decision became noticeably clear to Demetri, as he watched Cindy stand up and join a group of people close to her, that he must not be too anxious. He must be patient and methodical in his approach.

Demetri was pleased when he spotted it, "methamphetamine, my friend, has come to assist me!"

Chapter 2:
Indwelling

SHE WAITED PATIENTLY FOR THE PIPE to be passed her way. This would be her first time and she was a bit nervous, not knowing what to expect from her first hit of meth. But this was a time in her life she needed to let go and do the *wrong* thing. Cindy Firestone had never been what you would call outgoing in social settings. It was hard for her to make friends because she was so quiet. Her mind ran as busy as anyone around her, but her frightened tongue held her thoughts in place.

Void of many close friends she considered Angela Deed her best friend, and Angie, as she called her, knew all about what was in that glass pipe she had just grasped in her hand.

Angie placed the small butane lighter in Cindy's other hand and pointed at the pipe.

"Just bring it up to your mouth, Cindy. Take the lighter and hold the flame over here and just breathe in the smoke," Angie instructed as her teacher.

Cindy followed Angie's instructions and produced the drug laden smoke that entered her lungs. At first, she coughed profusely. She wondered how and why anybody would do this and feel this discomfort. Everybody

6

surrounding the campfire laughed with glee at the experience Cindy was having at smoking meth for the first time, and she felt embarrassed.

Cindy let the pipe pass from her hand to the other companions around the campfire. She watched intently as she witnessed the expertise that some of them showed in inhaling methamphetamine. Angie certainly knew what she was doing, and soon began to exhibit the effects of the drug, showing a heightened display of euphoria and sense of love for everybody around the campfire.

When the pipe once again came around to Cindy, she was reluctant to try again, but she was afraid to sever the social connection she was making with the other campers. As she brought the pipe to her lips, she clicked the lighter to produce a flame and began to inhale the smoke much slower this time. She wanted to feel what Angie was feeling. This time it went much better, and she was able to tolerate the smoke. Into her lungs the smoke proceeded and she passed the pipe to the person to her right.

Angie was so overjoyed with Cindy's success this time that she leaned into her and kissed her on the lips. Demetri was pleased. He wanted *this* Cindy as his host. In a way, he desired her, which felt strange to him. She would now be his, and he entered her.

At first, Demetri felt nothing unusual. This possession was just like most of his conquests before. He smelled the aromas of the campfire and her senses became his also. Then, he was abruptly expelled from her. He was on the outside looking in. This was different than anything Demetri had experienced before. Not one to give up, he focused his energy for another try. This time he felt her smooth young skin, he relished the racing of her heart. He had her mind and spirit. He was now in control.

With each inhalation of the pipe Cindy felt things she had never felt before — the love, peace, and feeling that she was a creature of beauty and desirable to her new friends. She was glad she came tonight and hoped this would be something she would do often. Despite the enthusiastic kiss she had received from Angie a few moments earlier, her friend had left her, and the campfire, with a boy named Josh. They had moved into a tent downwind from the campfire and Cindy could hear them laughing with each other until it suddenly became quiet.

She hadn't experienced sex but assumed that was what was happening in the tent they had disappeared into. Taking another hit off a vodka bottle that was passed to her, Cindy caught a glimpse of a boy smiling at her through the dancing flames of the fire. She blushed at the attention he was showing her and despite liking it, she still found it hard to look his way. She once again glanced into the crackling fire as she couldn't resist looking towards the boy. This time he was gone. Cindy was almost relieved he had moved because she found him cute, and the effects of the meth might have made her just bold enough to strike up a conversation with him. She leaned forward towards the fire and suddenly was startled by that same boy sitting down next to her.

"Hey pretty girl with the beautiful eyes, I'm Ben," the boy said in a seductive manner.

Cindy, in a shy and startled manner answered back, "Hi, I'm Cindy."

In an almost Victorian gentleman way, with his thumb and index finger, Ben tipped his ball cap to her and replied, "Pleasure to meet you, Miss Cindy."

Ben had produced a soda out of the front pocket of his hoodie sweatshirt and handed it to Cindy. "I went and grabbed you a soda. I know that sometimes *smoking the dragon* can make you thirsty."

Cindy was grateful for Ben's gesture because she was very thirsty. She brought the can to her lips and experienced a soda like she had never had before. The pleasures of food and beverage were not available to demons during a possession. Demetri wished they were, but to linger on the longing for these earthly pleasures would cloud his mission. Cindy thought the soda tasted wonderful and as she brought the can down from her lips she couldn't help but smile sheepishly at Ben.

Demetri really didn't like it when males got involved with the female mortals he chose to inhabit. He felt that sometimes they made it more difficult for him to deliver the *soul* by getting involved with his females' emotions. Still, there were times they could help make it easier. He just wasn't sure yet with Cindy. It was too soon in *their* relationship to know. He wished Ben would go away, at least for a while, so he could have more time to figure out what direction he would go with Cindy. The woman that he had taken in 1920 was just as beautiful as Cindy Firestone, but stronger willed. Still, Demetri liked this challenge and although there were also men in that woman's life, they certainly didn't manipulate her. That was Demetri's job.

"My name is Benjamin, but everybody calls me *Pipeline.*" Ben laughed in a nonchalant manner. "I guess I got that moniker because of my ability to supply everybody's pipe with the magic rocks!"

"Okay," Cindy acknowledged with a reluctant tone. "I think I'll just call you Ben."

Ben and Cindy continued to share trivial information with and about each other as the fire embers lit and danced in the summer sky. The pipe had become theirs alone, and Cindy listened intently as Ben instructed her on how to gain the most pleasure from her newly acquired hobby. As the night grew on, she became unaware that her abilities to execute a conversation with a boy had also grown. Cindy, with her newfound confidence had become somewhat of a flirt, and Ben had become the object of these flirtatious exhibits. As she laid on her back to take in the full splendor of the clear Oregon summer sky, she noticed that Ben had also laid next to her. Cindy looked up into Ben's eyes as he was now positioned over her. Ben leaned down to kiss her lips. All of this was new to Cindy. Despite being told by several of her family members that she was a pretty girl, Cindy had never really had a boy show interest in her. She often wondered if her alabaster eyes freaked them out.

After a few passionate moments of kissing, Ben stood, and reached his hand out to assist her up from the ground. Upon coming to a standing position, Ben wrapped his arms around her waist and shoulder and pulled her tight to him.

"My tent is right over there," he said as he motioned with his head tilting towards the tent.

She grabbed his open hand as he led Cindy down the beach away from the fire to his camping sight. This would be her first time. It wasn't quite what she imagined, and she certainly didn't think it would be with a boy called *Pipeline*.

As Ben manipulated Cindy in the experience of carnal pleasure, he looked deep into her alabaster eyes knowing that he had found a girl at this lake party to get lucky with. He had never been too picky, but for once, this conquest was a nice-looking girl and not one that had been smoking the dragon for a long time, and it showed. Cindy certainly was not what Ben had imagined he would hook up with tonight, and he wondered if she would still be this beautiful in a few months. Those thoughts passed from his mind as he continued with his business.

During these moments of sexual encounters, Demetri would retreat to the deepest corners of his subject's mind. He had no interest in this type of pleasure or pain unless he could use it for his own manipulation. In most cases, he would just ignore the process. Demetri mildly paid attention to this encounter since this sexual experience was new to this girl. This boy repulsed Demetri in every action he took with *his* Cindy.

As Ben neared completion of taking the virginity of Cindy, he lifted his head to glance into her open alabaster eyes. Just for a moment he thought he saw her eyes turn blood red.

Chapter 3:
Alex

HIS ALARM WENT OFF AT 3:45 AM, as it always does, signaling the time to end his peaceful slumber and begin yet another day of serving humanity. He was grateful to God for his job, and even though most people cringed when they heard what he did for a living, he was convinced that it was by God's design that he worked in the mental health industry. It was the type of work that certainly wasn't for everybody, and Alex knew that fact as well as anybody.

Alexander Dante reached across his queen size bed to shut off his alarm. He sat up on the edge of the bed, running one hand through his jet-black hair. Alex thought to himself that he easily could have laid back down in the coziness of his down comforter to try and grab a few more minutes of sleep if he hadn't needed to pee so bad.

"Oh well," Alex mumbled to himself, "guess I had better get up and move or this could well turn into one of those panicked mornings I too often have trying to get to work on time."

In the bathroom mirror Alex dabbed the remnants of the warm water he had splashed on his face. He folded the hand towel over the rack next to the sink and grabbed the hairbrush sitting on the shelf just above the towel rack. As he brushed his hair, he decided that it was nearing time to get a haircut. His thick black hair grew fast, he attributed it to his Italian heritage. He decided he would go on his next day off to get it cut.

His day-old beard lined his structured jaw and he jokingly flexed his right bicep. He had a muscular build and was fortunate that didn't have to work extremely hard to have it. His olive-colored skin revealed an almost perpetual tan that, based on where he lived in cloud covered Astoria, couldn't have been achieved from excessive sunbathing. Alex walked down the hallway from the bathroom towards his bedroom. He opened his dresser drawer to reveal powder blue medical scrubs. This was his usual attire for his job as ward attendant at the Oregon State Mental Hospital in Astoria. Slipping his scrub bottoms onto his six-foot three frame, he sat on the edge of the bed and laced up his gel cushioned insole tennis shoes. Comfortable shoes were extremely important in his profession since he walked seven to ten miles every shift.

With his grooming and dressing complete, Alex stared out of his kitchen window as he brewed coffee. His friends teased him for still having an old-school coffee percolator. But Alex liked his coffee strong and preferred the taste that only a percolating pot could offer. He poured the coffee into a Coleman thermos that had been handed down to him by his father. He packed a quick lunch of two peanut butter and jelly sandwiches, a small bag of potato chips, and he threw in a gala apple thinking he also needed something healthy.

Grabbing his thermos and lunch bag he tossed his Western-Oregon State University hoodie over his head and jolted out the door. Alex lived alone in a small one-bedroom house. The rent was reasonable, but even by Astoria standards as a coastal community, this place was a dump. Still, Alex loved the view that this little house offered. Directly west out of his front door you could almost see the entire mouth of the Columbia River and the Astoria-Meglerf Bridge that crossed the river and connected Oregon to Washington.

Having been born and raised in Astoria, this place suited Alex simply fine. He could not imagine living anywhere else. He could smell rain coming. Looking out onto the horizon he could see the clouds rolling in from the Pacific Ocean. He knew it would start raining by lunch time. Alex stuck the key into the door of his car to unlock it. Opening the driver side door Alex set his thermos and lunch box on the front seat. When he prepared to enter the car, and as he swung in his right leg, he caught a glimpse of something laying on the ground, just outside his car door, on the gravel driveway that served as such.

He was sickened, if not a little angry and disturbed by what he saw. This sighting had started to become a normal occurrence, based on how the neighborhood was becoming. Immediately, Alex knew he was looking at a syringe and a hypodermic needle.

Chapter 4:
The Ward

HEADING NORTH ON HIGHWAY 101 towards downtown, Alex thought about the syringe and needle he saw near his car. Drugs had become a real problem in his town, but they certainly helped contribute to his job security at the hospital. He could understand *why* people became addicted to drugs. Several of the patients he cared for in ward fifteen had, and were, still struggling with addictions. Drugs were an unpleasant fact and it disturbed him to think they had invaded the space where he lived. He was perplexed as to what to do about what he saw.

Should he notify the cops? There probably wasn't a lot they could do since it was just the paraphernalia. It was most likely just a transient passing by, and he hoped that was the truth. Alex turned onto Marine Drive where the Hospital was located. He glanced to his left and noticed there were only a handful of boats in the river today. A week before, the town of Astoria was rich with crowds of people, and in the water were more small fishing boats than you could count. All chasing the fall salmon run as the Chinook and Silvers migrated up the Columbia River to spawn.

It had been a good year for the salmon population and thus the anglers, and tourists were happy. The economy of Astoria reaped a huge benefit from the salmon run this year, but Alex was glad many of the people had come and gone, just like the salmon. He preferred a quieter pace and less crowds. He parked his car in the employee parking lot, grabbed his belongings, and headed for the hospital entrance.

The entrance had a single door with a small waiting area. A glass enclosure encased a small work area that housed a computer, a phone, and a control panel to open a heavy metal door that gave entrance to the hospital. All staff and visitors of the hospital were required to check in at this station and get clearance from George. George was a portly man that Alex guessed was around sixty years old. Alex was fond of George, and they often would take breaks together where he would share his robust percolated coffee with him.

"Good morning Mr. Bingham," Alex gestured to George as he scanned his employee badge and key card into the reader that allowed employees entrance past the *George* fortress. George laughed at Alex and replied, "Don't make me come out of my office and frisk you for contraband now!" Both men chuckled at each other as Alex saw the entrance door slide open. As he passed, Alex pointed at his thermos saying, "Extra strong this morning, Georgie."

George waived at Alex and replied, "Good boy! I need it strong today!"

Alex walked down the corridor towards his station at ward fifteen. There was another metal door that required special security clearance to open, and Alex had that authority. Ward fifteen contained nine rooms which housed patients. Two of those rooms were reserved for patients who had mental conditions, and were also either sentenced, or facing criminal charges. Alex was glad that currently those rooms were empty. He always felt that mental illness was no different for people that did not commit crimes, as those that did, but lately the inmates that had been coming to ward fifteen with criminal charges seemed more frightening.

Ward fifteen was *L* shaped with the two rooms that were reserved for criminal inmates immediately after their entrance to the ward. The other seven rooms, with three on the west side and four rooms on the east side, right after turning the corner. The inmate rooms were directly across from each other, and each had a metal door with a wired mesh window for observation of the patient. When these rooms were occupied, those doors generally remained open to the hallway, unless the patient was a *screamer,* which was not unusual.

Alex rounded the corner from the inmate rooms and glanced in their windows making sure that no new patients had shown up last night. He was relieved to find those two rooms empty and hoped they would stay that way today. The inmate rooms were numbered 15-1 and 15-2. Around the corner on the west side of the hallway was room number 15-3.

The door to 15-3 was slightly open and a thin gaunt man was lying in bed staring at the ceiling. Alex pushed the door open and came to the bedside and began to raise the back of the bed up to a sitting position.

"Top of the morning to you Mr. Sinclair," Alex smiled as he spoke. "The Queen will not be seeing you today due to the fact she has taken holiday at her country villa and wishes that you enjoy some very much deserved time off."

Steven Sinclair smiled back at Alex and in a very rough English accent replied, "Oh I do wish she wouldn't just spring these things on me. The Queen does know me best though, so I will just take my tea here in my room today."

Alex bowed and said, "Very good sir. I will return with your tea shortly."

Mr. Sinclair had been a patient at the Oregon State Mental Hospital in ward fifteen for over two years. All Alex knew about him was that he was delusional about being on the Queen of England's royal staff, and thought he was her personal assistant. Steven Sinclair was not even from England, but Alex enjoyed caring for him, and always treated him with dignity and respect. Sinclair trusted no one but Alex and would sometimes get distraught if he weren't there to care for him. Alex guessed it was due to the bond formed between a noble Englishman, and his valet servant.

Alex made his way down the hallway to greet and care for his patients in 15-4 through nine. Most of the other patients under his care suffered from depression to bi-polar disease and schizophrenia. The nursing staff and doctors relied on Alex and his muscle when patients were in their manic periods and required his strength to help subdue them. He had a reputation at the hospital for his ability to calm patients when they were experiencing rage. Many of the staff nicknamed Alex the patient whisperer.

Chapter 5:
Cocaine

SITTING ON THE FUTON with her butt barely on the cushion, Cindy leaned over the coffee table carefully dicing the cocaine into a fine powder on the piece of cracked glass she used to do her preparation. She pushed the masterly prepared powder into small, straight lines of perfect proportion, which would enable easy and effective entry up Ben's and her nostrils.

"C'mon babe, it's all ready, let's get high!" Cindy eagerly said as she motioned Ben to come sit next to her.

Demetri sat across the room stroking his left eyebrow and temple. Short stints when he did not indwell her were becoming more frequent. He was growing very bored and was finding these modern women very tasking. His memory kept reverting to the woman from 1920. She didn't seem to carry all the complexities this girl with the alabaster eyes did. He wondered if it might be easier to just take the torment, rather than suffer through the weakness displayed by this current muse.

Ben went first, using a small straw cut to the perfect length he inhaled a line of the fine powder into his left nostril, and repeated another line into his right. Cindy followed his lead and leaned back on the futon couch and closed her eyes to gain the full effect of the feeling of the drug.

She believed cocaine was her favorite drug. It's not that she didn't enjoy the effects of shooting meth or heroin, but *coke* made her feel better, faster. She was noticing that the other drugs were starting to require more and more of them to reap the same benefit of helping her escape. She needed to escape her life often, and cocaine helped her with that. She had moved into Ben's apartment based on his asking several months ago. That night at the lake had grown into living with and doing drugs with him. The pleasure she received from her recent inhalation was working for Ben also. Cindy felt him beginning to kiss her neck and reach up to caress her breasts.

Demetri, disgusted, thought to himself, "This is why I must sit here, opposite of all of this." His repulsion for this physical activity was beginning to grate on him.

In past possessions he could just retreat into the darkest caverns of their conscious when intimacy was occurring. It just didn't occur as often as these two seemed to engage in this activity. He wasn't sure why it bothered him so much, but he was sure it was because he despised Ben. It wasn't sexual pleasure that bothered him because he often used its perverted side to aid in the destruction of his host soul. After all, he had no sense of sex and would never know why mortals obsessed over it. Demetri wanted Cindy's full attention. He felt that she, for the short while he had her, belonged to him, and him alone. Ben was in his way, and he really hadn't grown tired of her, he was tired of Ben.

This realization made it much easier for Demetri to manage. As he witnessed the consummation of their act and as the two laid on the futon in their mortal nakedness, Demetri snarled and scowled, "Enjoy my host today, for tomorrow, you will enjoy her no more."

Chapter 6:
Escort

THE SMALL OFFICE AT THE END OF THE HALL of ward fifteen served as both a private area for the medical staff and a break area for Alex and George. George postured himself in a white plastic chair that adorned the room. Putting one boot up on the makeshift desk, he held his coffee cup up towards Alex's thermos to receive the robust liquid. Alex poured the hot coffee into George's cup.

"Holy Cow, George, don't you ever wash that cup?" Alex questioned.

George smirked and replied, "Nope, never have and never will. This is what makes the coffee taste so good!"

Alex shook his head at George as he poured the coffee into the discolored cup. Both men loved to tease each other about almost anything and George's coffee cup fit that bill. Both men sat and sipped their strong brew and George inquired about how Alex's day had been so far.

Alex answered, "It's been a typical day so far. The Queen gave Mr. Sinclair the day off today. Mr. Johnson complained the doctor screwed up his meds, and Andrea Best asked if I had reconsidered sneaking in some pot for her."

"Yes, fairly typical," George replied without changing the expression on his face.

The men finished the coffee and looked at the black and white circular clock on the wall which showed that their break time was over. They waved at each other as George waited for the door to open to allow him to exit ward fifteen and return to his post. Alex, unlike George, rinsed his cup out in the small sink in their breakroom and placed it onto the top of his thermos. He then put the contents in his small locker. As Alex left the breakroom, he could see the nurse was on her medication rounds and decided to escort her as she went from room to room.

He liked to escort this nurse in particular. Courtney Blair was his favorite, and he couldn't deny he had a *thing* for her. She was short, petite with straight chestnut brown hair that she always wore back with one ponytail. Alex couldn't recall a time that Courtney wasn't pleasant and friendly to him, even though she worked in the same place as he and faced the same patients and issues. By the way she spoke, and her personality that gleamed every day, he was certain she had to be a believer. Alex was cautious to never mention his faith in Jesus Christ to her since hospital rules strictly forbade discussing one's beliefs with other staff, and especially patients.

One day, despite knowing she probably wasn't interested in a simple ward attendant like himself, Alex hoped he could get up the courage to ask her out for coffee, or even better, a nice meal. One day he would get enough courage to ask her out.

"Good morning, Courtney," Alex said in a schoolboy tone as he came up from behind her to match her walking pace.

Courtney smiled back at Alex and replied, "Well Hello, handsome!"

Deep down, Alex knew that she didn't extend that greeting with any meaning behind it, but he certainly wanted to believe she did!

"Would you like some company on your med rounds?" Alex asked her in a sheepish and polite manner, trying not to seem too much like a puppy following its new master.

Courtney stopped her medication cart and looked at Alex and replied, "Would you do that for me? Ms. Best has been difficult lately about taking her meds. I know she *loves* you and might listen better if I bring her boyfriend with me."

They both laughed at Courtney's statement, but Alex knew she was only joking. Although Andrea Best often referred to Alex as her *boyfriend.*

Chapter 7:
Reconnection

PASTOR FIRESTONE HAD BEEN THE SPIRITUAL LEADER at Seaside Community Church for 31 years. The church itself had started in a storefront in the coastal tourist town of Seaside, Oregon with only twenty-five people including Glen and Margaret Firestone. Glen was a straightforward preacher. He believed the Bible was the inspired word of God and his messages from the pulpit were based on teaching his congregation that word. He believed that was the only way to bring people who were seeking to know his God. Many who came to his church were looking for more evangelism than Glen could provide, but he stayed true to who he was, and that was an old-time minister.

The Lord blessed the church after twelve years of struggling to keep it going and built it to what it was today. With a congregation of one thousand members, the church had been able to move into their new building, nineteen years ago. With the completion of the new church building, Glen and Margaret Firestone also welcomed their one and only child, Cynthia.

Glen was anxious as he sat in his church office. He stood to look out the window and stare at the traffic on the street in front of the church. He was finding it difficult to work on his sermon for Sunday, partly because he was excited that his daughter Cindy had agreed to have lunch with him on Wednesday, but the other part was that he felt guilty he couldn't tell his wife, Margaret. Cindy and Margaret had found it almost impossible to be around each other, and despite his counseling his wife to try to let issues go, she just wouldn't. He missed his daughter desperately, and he knew she would not agree to see him, if her mother was going to also be there. He felt ashamed to be deceitful to his wife.

When Cindy left their home over seven months ago, it had been exceedingly difficult on Glen. He needed to know his family was safe and she wouldn't divulge where she was going, or with whom she was staying. Since Cindy was over eighteen years old, there was not much he could do about it. She was a grown woman, but to Glen Firestone, she was still his little girl.

He had done his best to find out where she was staying through some of the young women at the church she used to hang around. He was distressed to learn that she was apparently living with a new boyfriend. This bothered Glen to the core of his belief and destroyed everything he had tried to teach Cindy growing up. If it were true, she was living outside of wedlock with a boyfriend it made him feel like a failure as a pastor but more importantly, a father. If that news wasn't enough to stress him, he also heard rumors that she and this young man were possibly into selling and using drugs.

It was by chance that he had run into one of Cindy's friends, Angie, who used to attend his church, at the grocery store. She said she knew how to get hold of Cindy, so Glen asked her to please have Cindy call him at the church. Glen waited almost a month and had given up on Cindy calling, when she finally did. He barely recognized his daughter's voice when she called.

"Hi, dad, how are you?" Cindy asked in a soft and almost inaudible voice.

Glen answered in an excited but careful voice, "I am much better now that I hear your voice sweetheart. I have missed you so much."

"I have missed you too, Dad. How is Mom?" she inquired in an earnest tone.

"Uhm, not so good, baby. She is worried about you. Let's not be concerned about us though, Cynthia. Are *you* okay, you don't sound so good?" Glen replied in a caring but concerned manner.

The conversation proceeded with Cindy telling her dad everything was fine. She had a job working at her boyfriend's business. As much as Glen wanted to pry for details, he decided it wasn't the time or place. A mistake his wife would have most certainly made. He inquired of his wayward daughter if she had some way he could reach her in the future. Not to pry or try and control her, but just talk to her from time to time. Cindy explained she did not have a cell phone, but her boyfriend would let her use his phone to call.

"Can you come see me honey? Maybe we could just have lunch and get caught up on your new job and try and start again," Glen asked in a hopeful manner.

Cindy agreed and said she would meet him at the church next Wednesday at noon. She knew she couldn't tell him the truth about her new job, or about her boyfriend. Her father would freak out.

"Okay, honey, I'll see you here at the church on Wednesday and we will have a nice lunch," Glen confirmed.

Cindy answered, "See you then Daddy."

As Cindy hung up Ben's phone, she placed it on the coffee table as he continued to sleep. She wasn't positive Ben would let her really use his phone if she wanted to call somebody. He was very protective of his phone and became quite angry if she used his property without asking. She knew why her father thought she did not sound particularly good. She was extremely high when she called him, but it was her only opportunity to get at Ben's phone without him getting *pissy* about it. Cindy picked up the bong that also sat on the table next to the futon and lit the marijuana in the pipe drawing the smoke up into her lungs. After smoking the entire bowl, she moved off the couch and stumbled into the bathroom.

Looking into the bathroom mirror she gazed at her alabaster eyes as they seemed more pronounced now with the dark circles that encompassed the skin below them. She splashed some water on her face and looked upon her naked features, calculating she had lost twenty or so pounds over the last two months. How could she let her dad see her like this, she wondered? Using her hand to scoop up water into her mouth from the bathroom faucet she was startled to see some blood dripping into the sink. Cindy looked up into the mirror to notice the blood was dripping from her mouth and lip. Reaching up to her mouth with her index finger and thumb on her left hand, Cindy was able to discover the source of the blood. With an easy tug of her finger and thumb she extracted her left canine tooth.

Cindy began to sob as she dropped the tooth into the dirty sink and collapsed onto the bathroom floor. With every heave and quiver of her sobs Demetri laughed. In her ugliness of the moment, he took great delight.

Chapter 8:
Realization

SHE WIPED THE TEARS FROM HER EYES and ran the outside of her hand across her nose attempting to disguise her distress when Ben opened the bathroom door.

"What the hell is the matter with you whore!" Ben barked in the most sarcastic and evil way possible.

For once since encountering this boy, Demetri liked the way Ben confronted her. It was pure evil, and he cherished evil.

Cindy sniffed and cried, "I'm upset, I just lost a tooth, and why do you need to be so mean? I just let you hump me you bastard!"

Ben scowled at Cindy, and as he turned to leave the bathroom he barked, "Well get yourself together quick because we need to go make a delivery! Geesh, and put on some makeup, your face is breaking out!"

Cindy picked herself up off the bathroom floor to shuffle into the bedroom to try to find some clean clothes or at least cleaner than most of them she owned. She found the one bra she had under the bed and as she put it on, noticed she barely needed to wear one at all. Grabbing the hairbrush on the nightstand next to the bed, she ran it through her hair to the best of her ability. Her hair was tangled and choppy, and she could have used a good long shower with shampoo and conditioner to make it easier, but she knew Ben wouldn't wait that long for her. This was a moot point anyway because she knew there wasn't any shampoo or conditioner in the shower.

As she walked from the bedroom into the front room, she could see Ben stuffing the packages with the rocks of meth and a small scale into a black backpack. As he finished, the last thing he inserted into his business pack was a loaded magazine that he clicked into place into his 9MM Glock handgun. It bothered Cindy that Ben had a gun and brought it with him. He explained it away that with all the cash they collected during a delivery, he couldn't be too careful.

"Did you wear your bra?" Ben inquired.

Cindy replied, "Yes, but I have gotten so skinny that I don't need it."

Ben reached over and grabbed Cindy's breast as if he didn't trust or believe her. "It's not for your boobs, it's like I have told you a million times, it's to stash the cash and drugs if we get pulled over by the cops. They will not check you out cuz you can press charges for that. The fact your boobs have gotten so flat is a good thing. More room in the bra," Ben smirked.

For the first time in several months Cindy came to understand she meant nothing to Ben. She was there to be his mule if things get dicey or when he needed to use her for pleasure. She needed him for the drugs, for without them, she began to feel sick. Just as all this realization came to her, Ben motioned her over to the coffee table where he prepared her afternoon injection. She wished she could just walk out the front door and never come back. Run to her dad and fall into his arms and let him hug all her sickness away. She wanted to cry but she would not give Ben the satisfaction of seeing her tears.

Cindy sat on the floor and took the rubber strap from Ben's hand and wrapped it tightly around her left bicep. As she inspected her arm for a protruding vein, Ben handed her the syringe and needle and she took it and inserted it into the bulging vein, then she injected the liquid that would make everything be all right again, into her bloodstream.

Demetri felt her eyes roll back up into her head. He wondered if she would be able to manage her medication on her own after Ben was out of the picture.

After a brief time, Ben grabbed the backpack and handed it to Cindy.

"C'mon, it's time to go to work. Pipeline needs to make some cash!"

Cindy threw the backpack over her shoulder and followed him out the door. The two figures walked down the lawn to where Ben's utility van was parked. Cindy climbed into the passenger seat as Ben crossed over to the driver's side. She placed the backpack on the floor by her feet. She needed it close just in case. Ben climbed in and started the van and placed the transmission into drive.

"Who is our client today?" Cindy asked.

Ben looked out to the side mirror as he pulled away from the curb and said, "Lil Satan."

Demetri let out a large demon laugh. He wished it could be heard by mortals.

"This *boy* has no idea. Today he will get to meet his true master for real!"

Demetri's master was *also* called Satan, but there was nothing Lil about him. This fool was expecting to purchase drugs from Ben and would also learn just how truly little he was. But first, Ben would learn that lesson. Then Cindy would be *his* alone.

Chapter 9:
Beads of Opportunity

TAPPING ON THE DOOR OF ROOM 15-5, the frail voice of Andrea Best beckoned Courtney and Alex to enter. Alex felt it best to enter first, and upon doing so, a large beaming smile came to the face of Andrea. She was a petite woman of fifty-five years with salt and pepper hair that had never seen a curl in its life. Most of the patients wore loose fitting cotton sweatpants with cotton V-neck scrubs as standard, but the hospital allowed Andrea to wear a plaid button-down long sleeve shirt over her top. Alex referred to her as his *hippy girl,* and she loved it when he called her that.

"Alex, my boyfriend, you are late in coming to see me," Andrea gushed.

Alex laughed and replied, "What, did you think I had gone and got another girlfriend?"

Andrea's brown eyes peered out from over the top of her wire framed glasses at Courtney. "Well, you seem to want to spend more time with her than you do with me. What's a girl to think," she exclaimed with a pouty mannerism.

Alex took the medications Courtney had prepared for her patient and sat down next to Andrea handing her the small plastic cup with the pills.

"Nope, you're the only *hippy girl* for me. Courtney here is way too educated for my tastes," Alex said as he handed her a cup of water to wash down her pills.

Andrea beamed a smile at Alex that he was certain came with a bit of a blush to her thin sullen face. Once the medication chore was complete, Alex explained to Andrea that he would be back very soon to take her for their afternoon stroll. She beamed a look of approval at Alex as their afternoon strolls had been instrumental in Andrea's improvement. It had been almost two years since she had last tried to end her life. Courtney could read in her chart that the doctors attributed this to finding just the right course and dosage of medications, but she believed that Alex might have something to do with her improvement.

They exited Andrea's room and closed the door. Andrea also couldn't always hear very well and liked to turn her television up when it was time for her soap opera.

Courtney touched Alex on the arm which he was sure was innocent, but it would certainly make his day.

"Thanks so much for helping me again, Alex," Courtney expressed to him in a kind and meaningful way, "Do you mind if I ask you why you call Ms. Best, *Hippy Girl?*"

Alex gave a little tilt to his head as he smiled at Courtney. He explained that during his walks with Andrea, she had told him that she had grown up a devout Catholic and she and her husband James, while he was alive, made their living making beautiful Catholic rosaries and selling them at the Saturday Market in downtown Portland on weekends. In addition to selling the rosaries at the market, Andrea's work and craft had become well known around the Catholic diocese in Portland, and she was commissioned by several priests, nuns and brothers to make rosaries for them. She loved making them and her work was becoming well known.

"Have you ever been to Saturday Market in Portland, Courtney?" Alex asked.

"No, not that I can recall," Courtney answered.

He explained that if she had ever gone to Saturday Market, she would understand that every hippy that had ever lived, went there to sell their goods! Courtney laughed at his explanation because Andrea certainly fit the bill as somebody that used to be a hippy.

"What happened to James?" she inquired of Alex.

Alex got a sad look on his face and explained to Courtney that James had been killed in a train accident several years back. Courtney once again touched Alex on his arm in a gesture of sadness. He went on to explain that the rosary that Andrea holds was a birthday gift she had made for James. "She hardly ever puts it down, and quite often you can see her sleeping while rolling James' rosary beads in her fingers. I will never ask Andrea to put them down. I am not Catholic, but I believe Andrea knows God. I cannot tell her my views, or I'll get in trouble, but Andrea knows... She knows," Alex said.

"You are a kind and special man, Alex."

Alex wouldn't forgive himself if he didn't seize this opportunity, though he was frightened beyond his wits. He walked Courtney to the door that led from ward fifteen, and as he waved his card in the reader to allow it to open, he asked Courtney in the most cautious manner he could muster.

"Hey Courtney, if you would like to see Saturday Market sometime, I would love to show it to you."

Chapter 10:
Arrow

SHE SAT STARING AT THE TELEVISION wondering why the girl in the soap opera hadn't left her sadistic boyfriend yet. In her right-hand Andrea could feel the smoothness of the rosary beads as her delicate fingers moved down the line of the beads. She came to the end and could feel the cross that she had at one time carved with precision and the decoration that adorned it.

She looked up from over her glasses at the handsome figure sitting on the wall radiator. Legs crossed with glasses that looked just like hers he mocked her by wearing exactly the same plaid shirt as her.

He spoke in a cynical way, "Why do you still *play* with your dead husband's beads woman? You know they did him no good! He serves my master now, not yours!"

Andrea Best showed him no anger and replied calmly, "Tell me his name, Demon."

"You know I cannot speak his name. My master would not allow it! And do not refer to me as Demon, I am an angel," he said with a bit of anger.

Andrea stared directly at him and said, "I know you cannot say the name of my God, yet. One day soon you will have no choice. You were an angel once Gayland, now you are simply a demon of Lucifer! I asked you to tell me *his* name. I know you cannot speak the name of Jesus. I asked you to say the name of my husband!"

Gayland cringed in pain at the name of Jesus. He stood to prepare a quick exit from Andrea's room understanding it was folly to have come. He just couldn't let this one go. She returned her interest to the final minutes of her show, but before Gayland could disappear from her presence, she shot one more verbal arrow through his demon heart in the form of the truth.

"You know not my husband's name because you did not know him in life, and you certainly don't know him in death. He belongs to Jesus," Andrea spoke.

With those words, Gayland was gone. Andrea took the TV remote in her free hand and shut off the TV. She must get in a little nap because a man of God was coming to take her for their afternoon walk.

Chapter 11:
Crimson Delivery

SHE HATED LIL SATAN MORE THAN ALL OF BEN'S CLIENTS. Every time there was a deal and delivery with him, she felt uneasy, like something would go wrong. Her instincts were clouded by drugs, but those same instincts always seemed to be on high alert when he was involved. Cindy just didn't trust him, and she wished Ben would not either. There were more than enough clients to buy his product without selling to Lil Satan. When they went out to do business, Ben required Cindy to call him by his moniker of *Pipeline*. If she slipped and called him Ben, there would be hell to pay later.

She asked as Ben drove, "Hey Pipe, why do you continue to do business with this idiot?"

Pipeline replied in a sarcastic way, "What the hell do you care who I do business with? As long as you get your *toot* should be all you care about!"

Cindy, sorry she said anything, turned her head to look at the scenery passing by her, "I just don't trust him is all."

Pipeline turned left on a side street that held the location of Bricks Restaurant. The side street next to the restaurant was where he liked to do his transactions. It wasn't suspicious to any traffic passing on the intersecting street, because Brick's parking lot wasn't large enough to hold all the cars of patrons coming to eat at busy times. Consequently, vehicles often parked on the side street. As he pulled a U-turn, he positioned his van next to the curb and placed the transmission into park. Pipeline continued to glance out of his side view mirror, looking behind the van with the intention of spotting Lil Satan's 1973 El Camino pulling up behind him to begin the business at hand.

"Go ahead and pull the scale out of the backpack," Ben demanded of Cindy.

She complied knowing it would be her job on the command of Pipeline to dispense the product into smaller bags based on the size of the order. She placed the scale on the floor next to the pack and repositioned the larger plastic bags containing the bulk of the drug that would net Pipeline all the money he needed to live on and carry on his business. Cindy wished she could smoke a joint right now to calm her nerves, but Pipeline hated doing business high, so she was afraid to ask.

"I think I see him coming," Pipeline called out as he moved forward in his seat to get a better look at his side mirror.

Cindy could see what looked like a grey colored El Camino coming down the street, and as it came closer, she knew their client had arrived.

Ben took the 9mm Glock from the seat next to him and placed it in the small of his back and tucked it inside his jeans. Cindy wondered if Lil Satan was such an upstanding business partner, then why bring a gun? All this added to her anxiety.

"You stay in the van, and I'll find out the quantity we will be filling today," Pipeline barked out his orders towards her. He continued with his directions, "Once I have his order you can exit the van and move to the back where you can fill the order, got it?"

She understood exactly, as it was the way they operated a hundred times before. Pipeline pulled on the handle to release the door and exited the van to greet his business partner who had done the same from the El Camino parked behind him. She could see Lil Satan approach Pipeline giving him a fist bump and a sideways *bro* greeting. Lil Satan was a medium build black man with long hair braided and flowing down his back. With his braided hair part down the middle, it almost looked like he had horns on both sides of his head. Cindy suspected that it probably had something to do with his moniker of Lil Satan.

Wearing a bold red t-shirt and Los Angeles Lakers leather jacket his smile revealed a solid gold grill inset on his teeth. Cindy realized those were new from the last time they did business with him.

"Waz up Homeslice?" Lil Satan inquired of Pipeline.

Pipeline answered, "Not much, LS. Just trying to make a buck out here in the mean streets."

Lil Satan shot a glance inside the van spotting Cindy sitting nervously in the passenger seat. "Ah good, you brought your little squeeze wit you today. She a whole lot more honest dan you is Pipe."

Cindy shot a nervous smile back at Lil Satan although it wasn't in pleasure or amusement. Lil Satan winked at Cindy and turned his attention back to Pipeline with a joking open-handed slap to his chest saying, "hey Pipe, wit whatever we do today on product, why don't you sell me your girl too. You don't take care of her like I can. You get me?"

Cindy found none of this amusing and she was slightly concerned that Ben might take LS up on his offer.

He turned his conversation back to Cindy saying "hey girl, he jackin you up on the crap he sells. You can still be one fine lady if you had a man that would get you off that crap!"

Pipeline was beginning to get annoyed with LS and his playing around, and he brought the conversation back to the business at hand.

"So how much you feelin today LS?" Pipeline asked.

Cindy was slightly relieved that the conversation had ventured from where it had been with her as the focus, and back to the drug transaction, but she couldn't help but have her mind wander to what LS said. What *if* she had a man that cared for her enough to never have let her get to the place she was today? A man like her father, who just cared for people, but without all the Jesus stuff.

LS answered "Well girl, you ever get tired of dis boy's abuse you come see me. As far as the *crap,* can you fill *fitty thousand* today?"

Pipeline nearly choked at LS's request. Fifty thousand would nearly wipe his supply out, but in one transaction he could finally take it easy for a while.

He answered his client, "I can fill it, but I'll need tomorrow to do it. How about half today and the rest tomorrow?"

"Deal," LS agreed as he pulled out his chained leather wallet and began to count out twenty-five thousand in cash into Pipeline's hand.

As he counted the cash, and distributed it to Ben, Dimitri was amused. He knew exactly *who* and *what* Lil Satan was now. He couldn't be more pleased that this was how Mr. Pipeline was going to be removed from his presence and delivered to his master. He became slightly worried that Cindy might come into harm's way when all this started to come down, and although that would reduce the amount of time to deliver Cindy's soul to his master, he wasn't ready to be done with her. With Ben in the picture, they had so little time together. Demetri determined he would flood Cindy's inner emotions with fear and concern causing her to know that something was drastically wrong.

Ben leaned into the driver's window and handed the twenty-five thousand dollars to Cindy. He impatiently instructed her, "bag up everything! LS bought the whole show!"

She didn't understand why she took the money and began to shove it in her bra. Normally, she never felt the need to do that, but for some reason today, she felt uneasy about this transaction and this money. With the drugs and the scale in her possession, it would be easy pickens for law enforcement to connect them with the cash, so she shoved it in her bra. Cindy grabbed the backpack to retreat to the back of the van and begin her job of transferring product to smaller individual bags for LS.

This was not what she had wanted the night she was kissed and lost her virginity to Ben. He was the first boy to appear to want her. None of the boys at her dad's church or at her school had shown any willingness to venture into sin with her. She had become so tired of the holier-than-thou life she was forced to live being a pastor's kid. Jesus had done nothing for her but made her bored. Still, this wasn't what she thought it was going to be either, and the hole in her mouth from the missing tooth was a reminder of that. As Cindy was distracted by gathering the pack with the drugs and the scale, she reached for the handle to open her door and was startled by car tires screeching with that awful sound they make when they are pressed into action to stop quickly.

Cindy, now on high alert, looked up to see several patrol cars with flashing lights pull up to the van to prevent any possibility of exit. She witnessed guns drawn with blue uniforms and brass badges descending upon her. The passenger van door was yanked open and large men with bullet proof vests and guns held towards her chest barked the command to get out of the van and lie on the ground.

Her first thought was to do what Ben trained her to do and shove the drugs in her bra and down her pants. The police were never in a position to search a woman, and by the time they might be, she could stash the evidence.

This time, there was nothing she could do, because her female areas were crammed with cash. Besides, as she was being pulled to the ground, she noticed that several of the officers in blue were female. There was no way she could escape the search that was to follow.

Cindy laid on the asphalt with her feet towards the van and her face pressed against the pavement as an officer brought her arms and wrists to be handcuffed together. It hurt and she wished they would hurry and bring her to a sitting position. She was curious if Ben and Lil Satan felt the same pain on the other side of the van. Just then she heard the words that brought why she felt anxiety earlier. Words that would forever change her life were barked by the officers, but she could not see on the other side of the van.

"Gun – gun –gun!"

The words echoed to and filled the fibers of her soul. Then several raps of gunfire followed. More voices yelled out in unison "he's down, he's hit!"

As Cindy felt the pain of a knee wedged between her shoulder blades subside, she tried to gain some perspective on what was happening. One of the officers that had been attending to her custody retrieved her radio and called dispatch "Code 61, we have a suspect with multiple gun shots down. We need EMT's dispatched with an ambulance to Sixth and Milwaukie. Scene secure."

She knew that the suspect the female officer was referring to was Ben. The gurgling sound from his labored breathing was without a doubt him. She sensed he was gone and could imagine police officers hovered around his bullet pierced body as his crimson fluid filled the street around him. Cindy knew he was gone and thought for a moment that the officer had only said *suspect*! What had become of Lil Satan? He must have followed the command to lay down on the asphalt pavement, and live to buy and sell drugs another day, despite being twenty-five thousand dollars poorer. Perhaps it wasn't even his money and was that of his boss, a drug lord that would bail him out only to kill him for getting caught. "How did they get caught?" she thought. Had she said something to somebody when she had used Ben's cell phone during his deep, drug induced sleep?

Cindy thought she should feel bad, even sad, for Ben. All she could think of is if she could even wiggle out of major drug charges from this event, how or where could she get her drugs from then on? Her only supply source was lying in a pool of blood in the street on the other side of the van. She needed Ben for the drugs. She was terrified.

Demetri was pleased. This whole thing could not have happened any better. He couldn't remember in his three thousand years anything happening this well. Pipeline was gone and off to meet his master. He laughed and cackled, "Pipe, my boy, sorry things didn't work out well with your meeting with Lil Satan, but I would like you to meet Big Satan!"

A female police officer helped pick up Cindy and get her on her feet. As they placed Cindy in a patrol car, she could look around her to see if possibly Lil Satan had been the one struck down and she could glimpse Ben being placed in a patrol car just like her. She knew it was a futile thought and she saw no sign of either of the men she had started this episode.

Demetri decided he would keep the truth from her. He was perplexed to know why he even cared. Yet, she had suffered enough today, and it would be nothing compared to the coming withdrawal she faced from the drugs. He could see Little Satan down the street from Brick's

Restaurant sipping a bottle of water and receiving pats on the back from his superiors in the Drug Enforcement Agency. Lil Satan would not be in jail today. Later, he would be sitting at the bar, drinking a beer, celebrating a large drug bust and supplier getting taken out. His friends and co-workers knew him as Detective Jamal Smith.

Chapter 12:
A Feeling

ALEX COULD SMELL THE RAIN IN THE AIR. He stood in the courtyard outside ward fifteen and watched the clouds as they rolled in. Rain clouds in the Pacific Northwest were nothing unusual, and in a way, he liked it when it rained. Somehow it brought a freshness and cleansing to the world even though it was a small world he lived in.

He took the last few bites of his sandwich and washed it down with some more of the coffee he had brought for himself and George. He wondered if it would start to rain before he could escort Ms. Best on her afternoon walk. He determined he would cut his lunch break a little short so he could try and squeeze it in. Alex enjoyed his time with Andrea. He knew she was a woman of God, and despite not being able to expound on his beliefs and perspective, he enjoyed listening to hers.

Since Courtney had left his ward to do her rounds in other parts of the hospital, Alex was sure the smile on his face would not disappear today. Ms. Best would certainly know something was up because despite no definite date being set, Courtney had accepted Alex's offer to go to Portland and Saturday Market with him. Andrea's *boyfriend* was in jeopardy to leave her for another woman!

Alex laughed aloud at this thought. He screwed on the cap to his coffee thermos and wiped his cup dry and headed into the employee locker area to stowaway his items. As Alex bent to put them in his locker he placed the padlock on the holder, snapped it shut and gave the dial a quick spin.

Standing up from his crouched position, Alex sensed something was odd in the room. He felt as though someone had been there watching him while he was putting away his thermos and remnants of his unfinished lunch. For a moment he thought it might have been George coming to get some of his coffee, but that idea was quickly dispelled because he would have had to buzz George into the ward. "Funny," he thought, "I could have sworn I saw the image of a man. It was only a feeling and shadows, but definitely a man. Well, it couldn't have been George, this shadow appeared tall and well built."

Alex shook his head and refocused on his duties at hand. As he started to exit the break area on his way to meet Andrea Best, he glanced back at the break room. Nothing but a couple of older, vinyl tables and a few white resin chairs. "Must have been too much caffeine today" he whispered to himself. Alex turned the corner and tapped on Andrea Best's door. A cheerful voice called out from behind the partially closed door, "Is that my boyfriend come to make our date?"

Alex pushed open the door and replied in an equally cheerful manner, "Of course it is, as promised!" Alex helped his Hippy Girl put on her sweater and watched as she buttoned it up. Andrea had dressed for the occasion in her blue jeans and black long sleeve tee shirt advertising Multnomah Falls, a local Portland natural attraction. She had sculpted her salt and pepper hair into one ponytail and had obviously put on eye shadow and lipstick.

"Shall we go my Hippy Girl?"

Andrea replied as she placed her arm in his, "Yes, we better go now for I feel it is going to start to rain soon."

"Very perceptive of you, Ms. Best," Alex said.

Both smiled as Alex guided her out of the room and the heavy pneumatic door that served as the last barrier to ward fifteen. The walkway area for hospital residents that were permitted to spend a little time outside was pristinely groomed with the grass nicely mowed and trimmed. During the summer months flower beds adorned the path and contained distinct types of annuals like snapdragons and daisies. Chinese Maples were prevalent in the landscape and there was no shortage of nicely trimmed Douglas Fir trees. It was noticeably clear to Alex that strolling along the walking area reminded Andrea of her days with her husband. She always held Alex's arm tight as they strolled, not because she needed his steadiness or strength, but because it made her feel normal. Normal to a happier day when she worked and walked with her earthly love, James.

Throughout the walking area along the pathways were placed benches so guests and visitors could sit with the patients that did not require escorts. Patients of ward fifteen almost always required escorts, like Alex. It had been some time since Andrea had attempted to take her own life and Alex suspected she might be moved out of ward fifteen soon. He was not allowed to discuss their diagnosis with anybody, including fellow staff members, but Alex had peeked in on her chart to discover she had been diagnosed with schizophrenia.

Andrea asked Alex if he would mind sitting for a bit so she could watch as the rain clouds rolled in towards them. As they sat, Andrea let go of Alex's arm in order to take the rosary that had belonged to husband James in her hands, and begin to move her fingers down the rows of beads. Cocking her head towards the sky she closed her eyes and began to say words that Alex believed were undoubtedly a prayer. He thought to himself, "If this is the behavior her doctors believed was schizophrenia, then he suffered the same illness."

He intently watched her as she mastered the movement of her fingers with the prayers of her heart, and he was incredibly careful to not interrupt her. After an abbreviated time, Andrea spoke "Amen", and turned her eyes back to her companion.

"Alex, do you believe in Angels?"

He was slightly startled by Andrea's question and was a little uncertain *how* and *if* he should even answer her. He had been reprimanded before by his superiors at the hospital for discussing his beliefs with patients. Despite being slightly concerned, he felt it would be wrong to not answer her.

"I believe they are created beings just like us," he spoke in an earnest tone as he looked directly into her eyes. "I believe they have powers and abilities that are different from us. In many ways, they are closer to God…than us."

Andrea studied Alex's face after his explanation, like that of a schoolgirl.

"If your question is leading towards asking me if…" Alex hesitated to the point he found it hard to speak. "If your question is, do I think that James is an angel, then, I am truly sorry my friend your question as *no*."

She let out a quick laugh which surprised Alex. "Oh, my dear, I understand that James is *not* an angel. He most certainly was a human. You answered my question in the manner I had hoped."

Then Andrea's face became a bit somber and serious. "If you believe in angels, my dear man, then you must believe in demons?" she asked.

"I really haven't thought much about it to be honest. I understand that there are fallen angels that chose to follow

Satan. What they do, and how they do it, I am not really sure." Alex answered.

"Why do you ask?" Alex quizzed.

Andrea motioned by moving her arm back to cradle within Alex's arm to take her back to her room. As the couple began their stroll back to ward fifteen, Alex felt small drops of rain begin to hit his face.

Chapter 13:
Gayland the Demon

HE HATED FLOWERS. Despite not being able to smell them or delight in their beauty, he knew humans felt joy and gave credit to their Heavenly God for their creation. Gayland could offer no credit for anything to Gabriel's God. Now that the spring and summer season had departed, and the damp coolness of fall was upon this place, he relished in the death of the foliage and the sun getting driven behind the clouds.

Depression was more frequent in the fall and winter times. Gayland found the humans that came to be at this Hospital were easy for him. As he dispatched one soul to his master, he need not travel extremely far to find another. Not that he was required to do so. Occasionally he would target a new soul only to discover one of his fellow demons were indwelling them and engaged to deliver their souls but finding another never seemed urgent.

He knew his fellow demons felt like Lucifer thought him lazy because he stayed here. He knew that most of the souls that came here would be delivered to Lucifer by their own accord. Failure in a demon's mission to deliver souls to which they indwelled, would usually lead to torment and despair as punishment. Gayland never needed to worry about that. He was always successful, except once. The rosary hag was his only failure. So close he had come. Now her presence at this place torments him daily of his failure. She once allowed him to penetrate her essence because of the love for her husband. Gayland had convinced her that he had the only way she could live an eternity with him, was through *his* god. So close he had come.

Now she belonged to Gabriel's God. He wasted his time then, and now, by trying to mock her. She no longer fears him when he visits, and now she mocks him. Gayland doubted that any soul had ever mocked Demetri. His master cherished the precious Demetri. Demetri the bringer of beautiful souls that had never turned to the God of Gabriel.

Gayland had a method to his madness by staying close to this hospital. Not only could he learn why humans choose the God of Gabriel, and from this knowledge, he would never fall into that trap to fail again. Never again would he lose a soul like Andrea Best. But he had a different mission that brought him here.

When he stood in the breakroom observing the human, Alex Dante, Gayland had almost made the mistake of letting himself be seen. Unlike the times he had visited Andrea to mock her, and to try and make his failure seem more tolerable, it wasn't time to be exposed to Alex. Still, this human and believer in Gabriel's God sensed he was there, and for a moment Gayland thought Alex could see him. "This is a mysterious and powerful human," Gayland pondered.

As the rain began to fall, he stood in the window of the room where mortals would gather to eat food and fellowship with each other. Gayland was intrigued by a machine that dispensed several different types of liquid refreshment. What garnished most of his interest was the ice-dispenser. Gayland wondered what it would be like to taste ice. He could not resist putting the ice in the glass and then pouring the liquid over it and watch it engulf the ice. How delightful this must be. Then his delight turned to anger because he would never know what this felt or tasted like. Even when he indwelled a soul, he wasn't allowed their senses of mortality or pleasure. Gayland set the glass with the ice and liquid down on the table. As he scowled, out on the pathway outside, he watched Alex and Andrea hurry back to ward fifteen.

Chapter 14:
Disappointment

IT WAS FAR PAST NOON ON WEDNESDAY and Glen Firestone sat at his desk with his head resting in his cupped hands. He moved in and out of prayer hoping that his only daughter, the pride of his life and soul, was just running late, or perhaps had just been delayed for a short while. He looked up at the clock on his office wall to see it read 2:35 PM. Reality set in that what had started out as a day of hope and excitement that he would be reunited with his child, was not going to happen. He stared at his phone for one last time, folded his bible shut, and grabbed his jacket to exit into the heavy rainfall pouring from the heavens.

As he went to shut the French doors to his office behind him, he realized he had left his car keys in his desk drawer. Opening the door, he moved slowly towards his desk and reaching around to only partially open the drawer to extract his keys, the phone rang. Glen reached to grab the receiver off the base and fumbled the handset back onto the desk knocking over a pencil cup with the action.

He recovered the handset and brought it to his ear in a hasty manner and spoke, "Pastor Firestone, can I help you?" There was a slight delay on the other end of the call when a female voice answered "Hello, is this Glen Firestone, father of Cynthia Firestone?"

Almost afraid to answer the question, Glen with his heart dropping replied, "Yes, I am Cindy's father."

"Mr. Firestone, my name is Investigator Harris with the St. Helens, Oregon, police department. I am calling to let you know that Cynthia has been arrested and is currently hospitalized at Mariners Hospital here in St. Helens."

"Is she hurt? Is she okay?" Glen asked in a frenzied manner.

"She is detoxing Mr. Firestone," Investigator Harris explained. "Cynthia is an extremely sick individual right now and she is in a whole lot of trouble. She is currently charged with several counts of possession with intent to distribute but she is also addicted to meth, heroin, and cocaine. Her doctors seem to believe she will be okay, but it will take some time."

Everything that Glen and Margaret Firestone had feared had come true. He blamed himself for his little girl being in this mess.

"What can I do to help her, Investigator Harris? Can I visit her in the hospital? I have to let her know I'm here for her!"

Harris replied, "Mr. Firestone, I will get you some information on when and where you might visit Cynthia, but in the meantime I would like to schedule a meeting with you and possibly your wife to sit down and find out what you might know or have heard about her activities over the last few months."

Glen paused a moment as he pondered the question he was just asked. "We would be more than happy to sit down with you and provide any information we can. Unfortunately, we haven't heard a word from our daughter in over nine months until last week. When would you like to meet Investigator Harris?"

"Perhaps this Friday at ten o'clock, at your church office? Oh, and please call me Pam."

He replied, "Fine, I will see you at ten, here at my office, and also please call me Glen."

As he hung up the phone, Glen could feel the tears come. He feared for his daughter's future, and he was helpless at this moment to do anything. His only recourse currently was to pray. Glen's head bowed and his torso leaned forward in his desk chair. As he began to pray, he sobbed.

Chapter 15:
Sighting

THE HOSPITAL CONTAINED A LARGE DINING HALL for patients that could function well enough to eat in a community environment. It also served as a visitor area so that families and loved ones could sit and stay connected. Alex almost never had any of the patients he cared for that were well enough to receive visitors at the dining hall. Not to mention that most of his patients seemed to be forgotten by their families.

He admired how nice the dining hall looked, with the beautiful lighting, black-padded chairs, and the beverage dispenser in the middle of the hall. He thought to himself that Andrea would be well enough soon to be moved to a different place in the hospital, and she could entertain guests in the dining hall. Not that he had ever known her to have a visitor in ward fifteen. For now, he could only pass by the dining hall, as he did after his afternoon walks with Andrea Best, as the pathway back to their ward went right by the dining hall.

Alex didn't want to push Andrea to walk any faster than they were, but he failed to carry an umbrella with him this time and the last thing he wanted was his friend to get sopping wet from the rain. Andrea kept her head down to absorb the raindrops falling as the walkway passed in front of the dining hall. Alex couldn't help but look up to get a glimpse of the dining hall through the large picture windows and see if any patients might be seated inside enjoying a visit with their guest.

Standing near the glass that looked out onto the walkway was a tall figure of a man. He had jet black hair just like Alex's, but it was slightly long and a bit shaggy in appearance. His eyes were dark. Alex thought they were as jet black as his hair. He adorned a black leather coat, the kind like a motorcyclist wore along with a black cotton tee shirt. This man was foreign to Alex as being on the staff, and he wasn't around anybody else seated in the dining room. His jet-black eyes studied Andrea and himself as they walked past him. For the moment that Alex noticed him, he would almost say he had a frown on his face. This bothered Alex to the point it freaked him out. What bothered him even more is Alex sensed he had seen him somewhere before.

Alex and Andrea reached the entry way that led to the hallway entrance to ward fifteen. He maneuvered Andrea through the doors and back to her room. Alex went into Andrea's bathroom and grabbed a towel for her to dry herself off. Handing it to Andrea, she thanked him for the visit. He didn't want to be rude to his friend, but he asked Andrea if she would mind if he left her to get settled because he needed to go check on something. Alex had every intention of returning to the dining hall to check on the man that stood so intently studying him and Andrea.

"Of course, I don't mind my dear," Andrea replied.

Alex blew her a kiss as he always did after their afternoon walks, and she blushed as usual. He left ward fifteen and headed back to the dining hall. He decided he would go up to the man and introduce himself and inquire if he were new on the staff, or could he help him find somebody he might be there to visit? Regardless, Alex felt uncomfortable with how the man was looking at him that he must find out who he was.

When Alex entered the dining room, he looked around the area to find nobody was there. All the patients and visitors had departed and left the dining hall until supper would be served. He could hear pots and pans clanging from the kitchen area that was contained behind two closed doors that would swing open as somebody entered or exited. Alex thought for a moment that the man was part of the kitchen staff. He really didn't know everybody that worked in the kitchen. What troubled him was that kitchen staff wore white jackets, not black leather jackets like this man.

"Oh well, I guess George wouldn't let anybody in that shouldn't be here," Alex thought.

As he turned to go back to his post at ward fifteen Alex noticed a full glass of iced tea sitting on the table by where the man had stood looking outside onto the walkway.

"Odd, he thought, it hadn't been touched. What a waste."

A few moments later after Alex had left the dining room to return to his duties on ward fifteen a portly man walked into a dimly lit dining room and walked over to where the glass of tea and partially melted ice sat on the table. The condensation formed a small puddle of water surrounding the plastic glass. He took a handkerchief from his pocket and wiped the water from the table as he picked up the glass. He examined the contents and smiled.

Drinking the fluid to completion he crushed a few pieces of what ice remained in the glass. He let out a small belch as he finished the beverage and George whispered to himself, "No sense in being wasteful Gayland!"

Chapter 16:
Understanding

SITTING IN THE CAR OF HIS GARAGE, Glen Firestone was pondering just how to confess to his wife, Margaret, the destructive news about the current fate of their daughter. She had to know. It would be deceitful not to tell her. Glen exited the car and walked to the back door. As he entered the house at the kitchen, Margaret stood at the stove mashing potatoes for the couple's evening meal.

Hi Glen, I'll have dinner ready shortly so we can eat, and you can have a moment to relax before leaving for bible study."

"I'm, ah, uhm, not going to bible study tonight." Glen placed his raincoat on the mudroom hook and put his bible down on the kitchen counter. "Jim Perkins is taking it for me tonight."

"What is the matter, Glen? You not feeling well."

Glen cautiously answered, "No not really. I'm not sick though, It's about Cindy."

Margaret's look turned from concern about Glen's health to one of despair. She placed the potato masher back into the pan and looked her forlorn husband in the eye and asked, "Please God, don't tell me what I have feared for so long."

Glen proceeded to tell her what he knew about Cindy's status. Margaret listened intently to everything Pam had shared with him.

"We must wait until Friday. Investigator Harris will be at the church office, and hopefully fill us in on how Cindy is doing as she detoxes. She also wants to interview us to determine what we know about how Cindy was involved with the drugs and this boy, Ben."

"But we didn't even know where Cindy was for the last nine months, Glen! And who is this Ben?" Margaret said with all the anxiety a mother could muster.

Glen replied, "I know, I know. That is what *we* will tell her. As for me, I will have to let her know I spoke to Cindy last week."

With a gasp of astonishment and anger Margaret scolded, "You spoke to Cynthia last week! I have been worried sick for nine months and you don't tell me!"

Glen diverted his eyes from Margaret. At this moment he couldn't bear to look at her.

"Cindy was to have met me today for lunch at the church. I was going to tell you tonight after I saw her. Honey, I love you, but God knows if I had told you she was coming, you would have wanted to be there, and you know that you and Cindy can be oil and water," Glen explained in earnest truth.

Margaret began to sob and turned from Glen and ran into their bedroom. He heard the bedroom door slam and he hoped it didn't crack the wood or break the door frame. Glen turned to the stove and turned off the burners that contained his supper. Without eating, Glen walked into his study, turned off the light, sat in a chair by the window, and stared at the rain falling.

When the morning came, Glen woke up on the couch in his study. To have said it was a fitful night's sleep would have been an understatement. He was certain that for as little sleep as he had, Margaret fared no better. He sat up on the couch and prayed. He prayed for Margaret and Cindy. If there was one thing that God had taught him all these years, it was that God was in control, and all he could do was pray for Margaret to find forgiveness in her heart for not telling her that he spoke to Cindy.

When he had finished praying Margaret opened the bedroom door. He cringed to think how she would react to him this morning and he thought it best to let her approach him in her own time. He didn't have to wait very long.

She stopped at the study door looking just a haggard from lack of sleep as he did.

"What time will the Investigator be at the church tomorrow?"

"At ten o'clock," Glen answered.

"We had better go early so we can pray in the sanctuary. I like to pray in the sanctuary, and it would be best if we did it together," Margaret rebutted.

Glen answered in an affirmative manner, "Of course, dear. Clever idea."

Glen decided to take Thursday off from going to the church. He worked on his Sunday sermon in his study at home, but concentration came hard. He and Margaret spoke extraordinarily little during the day and said nothing about the impending meeting coming on Friday. As Thursday night came, Glen was exhausted and hoped sleep would come easier tonight. At least for a few hours.

As Glen climbed into bed, Margaret was already positioned on her usual side. He thought it best to turn to his side with his back facing her so not to provoke her or solicit conversation. As he fluffed his pillow and settled in, he felt Margaret cradle his back and place her arm over his torso. He placed his hand on her arm and softly said, "I love you."

Margaret responded, "You have no choice."

Kevin Wollenweber

The two fell asleep holding onto one another and slept,
as angels watched singing praise to God in the highest.

Chapter 17:
Reckoning

SITTING IN THE FRONT PEW of Seaside Community Church Glen and Margaret held hands as they finished praying. Their prayers did not contain wants and needs, but rather strength and resolution from their Lord. For the first time that Glen could remember, Margaret pivoted in her seat towards him and began to discuss her relationship with Cindy.

"Ever since Cindy was young, I expected her to represent the type of child respective of a Pastor. I never let her do what other kids did. I never let her have fun. When she wasn't at church, she was home doing her schoolwork or bible study. I sheltered her from other kids so she would be the upstanding child that the church congregation expected. She never watched television or went to the movies with the other kids."

Glen interrupted, "Margaret, you mustn't beat yourself up over this."

Margaret quipped, "I was too caught up in appearances of being the perfect church family. The older Cindy became, the harder I pushed. The tighter I flexed my control. I didn't realize I was causing her to pull away."

She laid her head on Glen's shoulder and cried "It was me. This was my fault."

Glen let her continue to get all the pent-up sorrow out as much as she could. He knew that Pam Harris would soon arrive and perhaps a good cry would help Margaret settle herself. He also knew that she was having a breakthrough to understanding that by fighting every single battle with Cindy, her daughter had quit fighting, and simply wanted to escape.

They retreated to Glen's office to prepare for Pam Harris to arrive. Shortly after ten in the morning she arrived at Pastor Glen's office. Pam Harris was a petite woman of five foot one in heel shoes. She was sharply dressed in a blue blazer with gray slacks. Her hair was short but with a long wave bang. It looked styled and very current for an investigator and policewoman.

Pam Harris introduced herself to the Firestones who returned the favor. Glen asked Pam if she would be more comfortable sitting around a small table in his office and she agreed. Once they were all seated Pam started the conversation.

"Mr. and Mrs. Firestone,"

"Please call us Glen and Margaret," Glen interrupted.

Pam replied, "Thanks, Glen, I prefer these types of meetings to be less formal also. Let me start by saying that Cindy is recovering. She was a very sick girl and is not out of the woods yet with her addictions, but her doctors feel she will be okay with some time."

Both Glen and Margaret breathed a sigh of relief with this news.

"Pam, will we be able to go see Cindy?" Margaret asked.

Pam replied, "I wish you could, but because Cindy has received some serious criminal charges you won't be able to see her until she is booked into St. Helens Detention

Center. I will definitely let you know when you two can schedule a visit."

Investigator Harris proceeded to move the conversation to the reason she came to Seaside to speak with the Firestones. She asked Glen and Margaret if they knew anything about the person Cindy had been living with, which was Benjamin Tasker.

Glen became the spokesperson for Margaret and himself in answering Pam's questions.

"We have never met, or even know who this boy is. In fact, we hadn't spoken with Cindy for over nine months until she called me a week ago."

Pam tilted her right eyebrow at Glen's statement as she was intrigued by his answer but pressed on with her questions.

"What did she say when she called you? Did she call you at home and who did she speak with first?"

This question made Glen fidget a little based on the turmoil it had just recently caused them. He reluctantly explained, "Cindy didn't call our home. She called me here at the Church. We talked about how much we missed each other, and Cindy said she was working for her boyfriend's business. I didn't want to press too hard as I was trying to get her to commit to meeting with me in person. I didn't even ask his name."

"Did she agree to meet with you?" Pam inquired.

He answered, "Yes, we agreed to meet here at the church last Wednesday. We were going to have lunch and I hoped to learn more about her job and this boy. Cindy never made our lunch date and I heard nothing from her until you called me."

Margaret had grown fatigued just listening to the conversation and decided it was her turn to seize the opportunity to discover answers regarding what Cindy had been doing and with whom.

"Can I assume that Cindy and this boy, Benjamin, were living together and doing something illegal? What are Cindy's charges and was Benjamin arrested too?" Margaret pried.

"Fair questions, Margaret. My investigation has confirmed that Cindy and Benjamin were living together in a house leased by Mr. Tasker. As far as his *business*, your daughter has been charged with several counts of possession and distribution in addition to obstruction and illegal firearms. I suppose it's easy enough to figure out we believe they were distributing heroin, methamphetamine and cocaine," Pam advised.

Margaret looked at Pam with one of those looks only a mother can have. With her voice slightly cracked and barely audible she asked Pam, "Did the boy she was with, this Benjamin, get the same charges also?"

Pam's answer was delayed for a moment and then she sat forward and replied to Margaret, "No, Benjamin Tasker will not receive any charges."

Annoyed with that answer, Margaret, pushing on with the belief that she was due some answers in defense of her daughter, demanded, "Why would Cindy get all the charges and not this boy? He was obviously controlling the situation and manipulating Cindy!"

Pam quickly glanced over at Glen to read his face and suspect he desired the same answers as his wife.

"Folks, Benjamin Tasker is dead. He was shot and killed during a drug enforcement sting on Wednesday," Pam replied in as sensitive a manner as she could muster.

The Firestones sat very quietly and dumbfounded at the news they had just heard. Pam explained that since it was still an ongoing investigation, she couldn't reveal a lot of the details. They did not know this boy Benjamin, so it was hard to feel remorse for him. Still, they listened intently to what Pam Harris *could* tell them. She revealed that the reason she was there to interview them today was to try and learn if Cindy had revealed any information to her parents about Benjamin *Pipeline* Tasker's operation.

After an extended amount of questioning directed towards them, Pam Harris was convinced they didn't know very much, if anything at all. She continued to expose that she believed that Benjamin Tasker was a small fish for a much larger supplier. This sting operation was an attempt to capture Benjamin and hopefully get his supplier exposed. The small fish giving up the big fish scenario. Unfortunately, Benjamin had other ideas about getting caught and it cost him his life. Pam advised Glen and Margaret that it was fortunate that Cindy didn't make the same poor decision as he had.

She really did not feel that Cindy knew anything about the connections that Benjamin was using to get his supply. She relayed to them that she believed that Cindy had been a used, worn, rusty, neglected tool in the hands of a man not fit to wield it. In the past he had been notorious for using girls to help him in his distribution of the drugs by getting them hooked since he had easy access to the most addictive substances and used them to help measure, package and collect the money. Women were essential in any distribution operation because they could hide drugs or cash and were least susceptible to search by law enforcement. What Pam told them then made them both feel ill.

"Benjamin was known to use these girls for his own pleasure and that of his *customers*. I'm sorry to have to tell you this but I didn't want you to start feeling sorry for this guy."

Any feeling of remorse for this boy had long since departed for Glen and Margaret. Pam began to wrap up her interview with the Firestones and felt she had received about all the *intel* she could get from them. It appeared to her that Cindy was a victim in Benjamin's operation. A *willing* victim, but a victim, nonetheless. As Pam stood to begin her departure, she assured the Firestones that she would let them know when Cindy had been moved to the detention facility and to the best of her ability, she would try to paint Cindy as a pawn and victim in order for the District Attorney to reduce Cindy's charges.

She told them as she departed "I would get Cindy a lawyer if you can. Perhaps a good lawyer could reduce any jail time she might have to spend. I would definitely encourage her to try and put this all behind her as soon as possible, God willing."

Glen walked Pam to the exit from the church and after she departed, he turned to see Margaret standing behind him. He walked up to her and placed his arms around his wife and held her until neither had the strength to hold up the other.

Chapter 18:
Sun Dial

THE SUN BEGAN TO CREEP ACROSS the white marbled floor of Cindy's room. She watched the illuminated square box that was formed from the lone window of her room at the detoxification center. The fact that she could keep her eyes open for *any* length of time delivered to her battered heart some sense of hope. At least the nausea and pain of her detox journey was beginning to subside. It could have been better if she hadn't been shackled to her bed.

Her attention was distracted away from the makeshift sundial advancing across the floor of her room and onto the man sitting along the wall. Through the slits of her partly opened eyes, she could see he was a cop. He wore a nicely pressed blue uniform and she could see the brass badge he adorned on his shirt. His nicely polished black boot was elevated off the floor and resting on a small table placed in front of his chair. Cindy could see his attention was directed towards some kind of electronic device which she suspected was a tablet.

"I must be a pretty boring assignment," Cindy called out with as much voice as she could manage. The cop looked up from his tablet upon hearing Cindy's voice.

"Hello there, young lady. Welcome back to the world."

She could tell he was an older gentleman but unlike some older cops had not let himself go. He was physically fit and took pride in his appearance.

"As far as boring assignments, I've had much worse."

Cindy responded with the obvious question, "How long have I been here?"

Demetri knew how long she had been there. In a way it had been so boring for a demon that he wished she might have died, so he could hand her over to Lucifer and move along. He stopped himself from having those thoughts. He was still intrigued by her, and really wasn't ready to relinquish control of her soul, just yet.

"You have been here about three weeks, Miss. My name is Officer Banner. I'm with the St. Helens police department."

Cindy asked, "Can you undo the shackles on my ankles?"

Officer Banner responded, "No such luck Miss, you are in custody and as long as you are such, I must leave those on."

"I guess I'm in a Hell-A trouble then," Cindy said as she brought her one free arm up over her face to cover her eyes.

Banner smiled at Cindy and replied, "Yes Miss, a Hell-A trouble."

Chapter 19:
Fire and Ice

WITH CINDY RESPONDING TO TREATMENT and beginning to recover to the point she had a clearer mind, Pam Harris paid a visit to Cindy and filled her in on everything that came down on the day Ben Tasker met his maker. Cindy listened and expected Pam to ask her questions about what she knew about Ben's operation, which she honestly couldn't answer. She did not know where the drugs came from, and Ben wouldn't have told her.

There was a time when Cindy cared for Ben, but those feelings were long passed, and in a way, she was relieved he was gone. After all, he really didn't love her, and if he hadn't been true to his name as the pipeline for her to feel good, she would have left him a long time ago. From the start, on that first night at the lake, she used him as much as he intended to use her. That is the truth she told Pam Harris. He embodied everything her parents kept from her growing up. He was her escape from the goody-goody life. He provided her the fun and *evil* that Glen and Margaret Firestone worked so hard to keep from her.

Pam sat and listened intently to what Cindy had to say. She was curious about the statements Cindy was offering.

Demetri was pleased at her words and laughed uncontrollably. "This is the girl I have been waiting for. At last, she sounds more like my girl from 1920!"

"How do you feel about your parents now, Cindy?" Pam inquired.

Cindy answered in a slow and calculated manner, "Now, I miss them."

Demetri's laugh subsided and the expression on his face turned to concern. Human connection to family usually never yielded satisfactory results for a demon.

Pam glanced over at a pitcher of ice water sitting on a bedside table next to Cindy's bed and asked her if she would like a drink. Nodding her head, Pam Got up, poured her a cup of water, and handed it to her and spoke in an almost motherly tone.

"I suspect they will be moving you soon to the detention facility. I can let your parents know when you are moved so they can schedule a visit to see you. If you would like me to do that for you?"

Cindy, once again, nodded. Pam grabbed her notebook and began to head towards the door to motion Officer Banner to return to his post inside Cindy's room.

"I expect the District Attorney will not be too easy with the charges against you. I believe you really do not have anything to offer us in *who* Benjamin was working with, and because of that fact, she will not cut you any deals. If you should remember anything important, like names, let Officer Banner know and I'll be right here."

Cindy knew she had nothing to offer to buy her way into a reduced sentence. All she could do was hope her dad might be able to help as he had so often in her life. Like the day she spoke to her father on Benjamin's cell phone, she wished her dad could take her away and use his God to protect her.

Demetri felt his grip on Cindy's soul further loosen and was irritated by his surprising inability to squeeze more tightly. He wasn't at all enjoying these thoughts she was having. He determined drastic measures must be used to better his position. His demon concern was validated when the very next morning Officer Banner informed Cindy she would be moved to the St. Helen Detention Facility that morning. It was not what Demetri wanted because Gabriel's God was active in that place, and it made it harder for him to accomplish his work.

He decided he must do something to alter this destination and do it quickly. As he pondered his options, another blue uniformed officer entered Cindy's room holding leg and body chains and advised officer Banner that Cindy would be transported to the jail immediately. Cindy was released from the shackles which held her to the bed and helped to her feet by Officer Banner and the transportation officer. Cindy felt a little dizzy. She hadn't been on her feet awfully long in the last few weeks and the blood rushed from her brain.

She almost fell to the ground and if it hadn't been for the officers and their assistance, she would have gone down. The leg and waist restraints did not help movement either and in what seemed like an eternity, Cindy was finally in the transport van and on her way to the jail.

As the van moved slowly out into the through-way that would take her to the St. Helens jail, Demetri became uncomfortable. Cindy sat next to another woman that was destined for the same facility. This woman was friendly and seemed to find it quite easy to strike up a conversation with Cindy. It wasn't the fact that this other woman was friendly and talkative, but what bothered Demetri was she held a black bible in her lap. This is exactly what concerned Demetri the most.

The girl with the dyed red hair that was shaved to the skin on the right side of her head smiled at Cindy as she spoke, "My name is Angel. Were you detoxing sweetheart, or did you O.D.?"

"Probably a little bit of both," Cindy smiled back at her as she answered.

'My name is Cindy, Cindy Firestone," she added.

"Are you facing some pretty heavy charges?" the red-haired girl inquired.

"Yes, I suppose I will be. All drug related. I will find out more once I'm booked in at the jail," Cindy replied.

"You got a man on the outs or is he in too?" Angel asked.

"That *man* is the reason I'm in this van," Cindy retorted.

This statement irritated Demetri because *he* was the reason she was here! Ultimately, he had always been a jealous demon.

"I'm sure he still loves you. I can tell that drug shit beat you up pretty good girl, but you will get pretty again. He won't be able to resist you when you pretty again," Angel said in a sincere way.

Cindy gazed out the window of the van looking at the rain staining the windows. She brought her attention back to Angel and softly answered her observation.

"Thank you for saying I will be pretty again, but he will never see me again. He is dead!"

Demetri had grown tired of the conversation and watching the beads of rain travel down the van windowpane through Cindy's eyes, he longed for more time at the lake. He hoped his master would reward him in that manner when he delivered her soul. His gaze was diverted from the droplets of rain back to the women's conversation when it struck him. Demetri gazed upon the arms of Cindy's new friend and was intrigued by what he saw. On Angel's forearms were small *cuts* and *scars* that had been formed from all appearances, by self-infliction.

Angel sincerely expressed how sorry she was, but Cindy calmed her embarrassment by telling Angel that aside from the need for the drugs, she wasn't sad that Ben's life was over. As the girls continued their conversation, Cindy could not help but notice the scars from cuts on Angel's arms. She felt comfortable enough in their newfound friendship to ask Angel about the markings. Why she felt this comfortable with this girl she didn't understand.

Angel, if you don't think me too pushy, and if it's none of my damn business just tell me so, but I'm curious about the scars on your arms?" Cindy quizzed?

Angel replied, "No big deal, you askin' bout my cutting. Lots of people want to know *why* I cut. Mostly, I get asked that question from every psychiatrist I ever have seen. I suppose the answer is I get sad. I get sad a lot. When I cut, it makes me feel better."

"Makes you feel better?" Cindy questioned with great curiosity.

"Yeah, it don't really hurt, believe it or not. When I cut it makes me feel like I am in, you know, like I'm in control. I don't feel that way when I'm sad. Just like when you get high, it takes you away from the pain. Funny how something that is supposed to hurt, feels good, huh," Angel chuckled.

Somehow all this made sense to Cindy. Demetri loved it. He liked this red-haired girl even though it was too late for her soul. She couldn't be touched because she belonged to Gabriel's God.

"So, is cutting yourself a crime? Is that the reason you are going to jail?" Cindy inquired.

Angel responded, "Oh heck no! Not as far as I know it ain't. I'm going to jail for murder one!"

Cindy was flabbergasted by Angel's response. "Murder!" she gasped.

Angel told Cindy her story. She had been raised by her mother but no father. Her mother had several men come in and out of their lives. Most of the men were drunks, or just worthless, but her mom always needed a *man* around. When Angel was seventeen her mom invited a new man to come stay with them. This one seemed different. He was kind at first and didn't drink or do drugs. He took good care of her mom, and despite the continued bouts of depression Angel suffered, he showed compassion and patience with her.

All of that changed on her eighteenth birthday. Despite the fact she was having a special birthday in her life, Angel was feeling extremely sad that day, and sleeping was all she wanted to do. She wanted to be alone and dwell in her sadness. Apparently, mom's boyfriend believed he had a better way to make her feel better. This was the first of many encounters with this man and all were forced upon her. It drove her even deeper into her sadness and increased the times she gained relief from cutting herself. Her mom became increasingly angry at Angel's cutting activity, and she decided she must finally tell her mom about the *attention* she was being forced to accept from her boyfriend. Instead of receiving compassion and then anger towards this jerk, her mom blamed Angel.

That was when Angel decided she must put an end to this pain herself.

Early one morning, when he came to Angel's bedroom, she waited until he was on top of her and she introduced him to her favorite razor blade. The police responded to her 911 call. They discovered mom's boyfriend with precision cuts to his throat that even Angel was impressed by. Those cuts were not self-inflicted upon herself like usual, but they still made Angel feel better, for a while.

With an emphatic voice Cindy replied, "I'm glad you killed him." Her words were cold and displayed a sense of someone who had become hardened towards the world. "Why do you carry the bible around?" she added.

Angel scratched her nose with a hand that could barely reach it and thought about her response very carefully.

"While you were barfing and crapping your pants at the hospital, I decided I had endured enough pain and cutting wasn't cutting it anymore," She giggled as she spoke.

"I tied a trash bag I stole from the cleaning cart in my housing unit at the jail around my head, to try and suffocate myself. I got real close to success but another girl told the guard. I guess I quit breathing for a short time because I am fairly sure I died. That is when I met him."

"Met who?" Cindy quizzed.

"Jesus!" Angel answered excitedly.

Demetri cringed at her answer and was determined this would not be the fate of *his* subject. He then realized that none of the cuts on Angel's arms were new. They were healing and soon they would be faint scars of a practice long since abandoned. There would be a different ending for Cindy. She would not hold a black bible in her hand and find peace in Gabriel's God.

Chapter 20:
Seizure

THE CELL PHONE WAS VIBRATING on the kitchen counter as Glen grabbed it. Caller ID showed a private number, and he was almost prepared to let it lapse into voicemail, but something told Glen to answer the call.

A voice came on to say, "This is a collect call from the St. Helens, Oregon Detention Facility. The call you are receiving is from inmate *Cindy Firestone.*"

The voice went on to explain the base charges that Glen would be incurring to accept the call, but frankly he didn't care if it cost a million dollars. This was his baby girl on the phone, and he just wanted to say, "I accept," so he could hear Cindy's voice. When he finally made it through the recording to accept the charges, he heard a voice on the other end he had waited for what seemed like an eternity for.

"Hi Daddy, it's Cindy," she softly said.

"Baby, how are you? I have waited so long to hear from you," Glen replied as he wiped a tear flowing down his cheek.

Of course, Glen had quite a few questions for Cindy, but he held back many of them in order to not overwhelm her. Despite her continued apology, Glen couldn't help but feel that she sounded so much better this time around.

"You don't need to apologize sweetheart. You sound a hundred times better than last time. Do you know what is going on with your situation, I mean, if and what they are going to charge you with?" Glen inquired.

"Daddy, I have several charges against me, and I really don't understand them all. Can you set up a visit with me so I can talk about what I am going to do? I don't know how Mom feels about me right now but maybe she could come too. If she wants."

"Your mom loves you the same today as when you were born sweetheart. I couldn't keep her away from coming to visit you."

Glen hung up the phone rejoicing and giving thanks to God that his daughter was safe even though she was in jail. He phoned Margaret right away after speaking to Cindy, to fill her in on where things currently stood. Margaret offered to set up the visit appointment and contact a friend that was a lawyer who also attended their church. They hoped that he could shed some light on how to proceed with Cindy's case.

By late that afternoon, Margaret had already set up a visit with Cindy at the jail in St. Helens for the next day at six in the evening. She called and made a hotel reservation at a local St. Helens Travelodge near the jail. She didn't think Glen would mind the expense due to the travel distance between Seaside and St. Helens, and she was sure the events of the day would require them to stop and catch their breath, in a manner of speaking.

As Margaret hung up her phone with the Travelodge, Glen walked in the front door. They embraced each other and tears of joy stained both of their faces. She filled Glen on their plans, and he was elated to hear the visit was available so quickly. He understood he would have to adjust his schedule at the church, but nothing mattered more than seeing his child.

She informed Glen that she spoke with Jim Turner, the lawyer that attended their church. He advised Margaret that he specialized in personal injury cases, but he would find out about Cindy's charges and could offer a referral to a criminal lawyer if they desired. Margaret and Glen knew it was at least a start to putting this nightmare behind them.

That night, after the whirlwind events of the day had come to rest, Glen and Margaret pulled down the comforter on their bed and crawled into their respective sides of the mattress. They came together and held each other and prayed. They prayed for Cindy and asked God to protect her. Despite being exhausted from their day, they kissed each other passionately for the first time since Glen could recall. That night, they made love, with spirits even more tightly intertwined than their bodies. The Trinity of their beings, body, mind, and spirit, were united as God meant them to be.

The drive to St. Helens Detention Facility was mixed with the usual Oregon rain. It was neither pouring nor a sprinkle, but just that steady fall that seemed as though it would never stop. As they neared the end of their journey from Seaside to St. Helens, Margaret received a phone call from Jim Turner.

"Hello Margaret, I know you and Pastor Glen are on your way to see Cindy, and I want to bring you up to date on what I discovered."

Margaret flipped her phone onto the speaker so Glen could hear. Jim walked them through the five charges, mostly possession and intent to distribute illegal drugs. Four of the five charges were felonies with one being a misdemeanor.

"I'll be honest with you; Cindy is in a lot of trouble. These charges are showing $250,000 to bond her out. That would mean $25,000 to you guys through a bail bondsman," Jim advised Glen and Margaret.

Glen's laugh to that information was strained and worried. "Gee Jim, I'm not Billy Graham. I don't have that kind of money available!"

Jim rebutted "Well Glen, some bondsmen will take a lien on personal property like a house or something like that, but I can't speak for them. Best thing to do would be to call a bail bondsman and talk to them. I also consulted with a friend of mine who is a criminal lawyer, he said that since Cindy has no prior arrests, he might be able to swing a deal with the prosecution, but she is for sure looking at some jail time. Unlike me Pastor, he won't be cheap."

Glen thanked his friend for the effort he put forward but when he hung up with Jim, he could see the concerned look on Margaret's face.

"I just don't know what we are going to be able to do to help her, Mag."

Margaret shook her head in affirmation though she still hoped for a miracle. Glen watched as the sign that read St. Helens, ten miles, passed on his right. He worried how he would deliver the news to his daughter, and imagined in some way, she would blame him.

If the worries about her case and his lack of money to help her were not enough, Glen glanced down at the black leather bible lying on the console of his SUV. "They probably won't allow me to give her this bible either," Glen muttered under his breath.

Cindy's mood was vastly different from her parents. She sat on her jail bunk with the tingling nerves of a child on Christmas morning.

Demetri was annoyed by how much Cindy's spirits were lifted. It was foreign to him to understand human absence.

It had been close to a year since she had seen them. She recognized her physical appearance might frighten them as it had changed drastically since the last time they saw her. Still, she missed them so she hoped they could understand how hard the drugs had been on her body.

If being aggravated at her jovial mood wasn't enough, Demetri didn't understand what to expect since this would be his first-time going face to face with somebody that preached about Gabriel's God. He had taken on clergy and priests before, but none of these foes had been *connected* to a host like this man and his wife. He pondered just how he would confront this dilemma.

Cindy looked up at the clock on the wall above the deputy's station in her inmate housing unit. It read 5:30. She sensed her parents were already at the jail and were checked in. She knew she wouldn't be able to hug them and feel her father's gentle assurance that everything would be okay, but just to see her mom and dad through glass and hear their voices on a phone would be enough.

Demetri felt something he never recalled feeling before — panic. He did not understand this mortal, human feeling at all, and he was certain it wasn't because his host was feeling this way. Her human father didn't even cause him to feel this way. In fact, he was curious what it would be like to meet him and hear the lies he told. All he could sense was that his anxiety was being caused by being *in* this place, in this jail. Cindy was getting exposed to Gabriel's God way too frequently for his liking. The answer was to get her back to an environment that he could be more in control. Somewhere, where Gabriel's God was not so prevalent. Then it came to him. He was far more in control when Cindy was in the hospital. He must find a way to get her out of here and back into a hospital where it would be so much easier to deliver her soul to his master.

Cindy sat at the dayroom table in front of her cell waiting for the deputy to announce she was moving to the visit area. She was nervous but also excited. She looked up at the clock once again, but as she did, she felt a warmth come over her. The next thing Cindy saw was an EMT kneeling next to her placing an oxygen mask over her nose and mouth.

"Just lay still, miss, and breathe in deep. Tell me your name?" The EMT asked.

"No wonder I find such favor with my master," Demetri thought with an arrogant internal tone. "She will have no visit tonight. This seizure will buy me the time I need to plan her departure from this place."

Chapter 21:
Reunion Lost

As the lobby deputy walked towards him, Glen could see the expression on his face bore unwelcome news. Deputy Anderson introduced himself to Glen and Margaret and explained that Cindy had suffered an apparent seizure which was unfortunately normal for people who are coming off drug use and would not be able to make their visit. He apologized to them for the inconvenience and advised them to check back in the morning to hopefully learn of Cindy's status.

"Do you know if she is alright?" Glen asked the deputy in a concerned but frantic way.

Deputy Anderson replied, "All I can tell you is what I know. She is coherent and is awake. Medical has responded and she is receiving the best care available."

Deputy Anderson handed a business card to the Firestone's with all the numbers they could call in the morning. Margaret looked at Glen with the expression that this would be another one of those longest nights of their lives.

As they collected their belongings to exit the jail and head to their car, Glen spoke to Margaret, "Mag, we must have faith that Jesus will be with her and protect her. This is Satan's work, and he delights in challenging us."

Glen's statement at that moment could not have been truer.

A nurse shined a small flashlight in Cindy's eyes to follow her pupils. Cindy sat up on an examination table in the jail medical facility and tried to gain some focus on her surroundings. As difficult as it seemed for her to be able to speak, she did her best to ask if they knew the status of her parents.

The nurse explained to Cindy in a slow and methodical manner that she had a seizure and if she had a visit scheduled with her parents, they had been told and could reschedule. Cindy understood what the nurse was telling her, and tears began to flow out of her alabaster colored eyes. After some fluids were administered, the nurse advised Cindy she would be staying in the medical unit that night. Her vitals were improving, and the nurse did not deem it necessary to have her transported to the hospital.

Despite hearing the news that her condition wasn't serious and in fact very normal for a drug addict, that information provided her no relief. She had looked forward to being reunited with her parents and now that moment was lost.

Demetri was not excited over the prognosis either. His plan was successful to get in the way of Cindy's reunion, but it would not fully remove her from this facility and all the options available for her to *recover* and make his job much more difficult.

"No, this will not do at all. My master trusts me to do a better job than this! Somehow, I must produce a way to cause my mortal to *need* to leave this place," he pondered with some unfamiliar anxiety.

Then, it came to him, and he was certain it would be his best work ever! Demetri stood in Cindy's quiet room, as the medical staff had left her sedated. The only light that showed was a small nightlight and the medical unit that contained the tubes and probes that were attached to Cindy to display her vital numbers for the medical staff to track. The minimal glow outlined the magnificence of Demetri's body. The muscles of the Adonis to which he represented. His physique began to transform and become something else.

Cindy's eyes were hardly open. Through the slits that were manifested by sleep, and grogginess, she tried to gain focus of the figure standing by her bedside. "Daddy is that you?" she cried out.

The figure reached out and took Cindy's hand. As her focus became better and she could squint to try and overcome the lack of light in the room, her recognition of who or what the figure was, became clear. Cindy gasped at *its* presence.

Standing by her side, clinging on to her hand, was a smiling Benjamin Tasker.

She was shocked by his presence and choked on her words.

"Ben... I mean *Pipeline*, I-I thought you were dead. I saw you laying on the ground. You were shot," Cindy said with a barely audible voice.

He replied with the utmost sympathy, "I couldn't leave you alone. You need me. Who else is going to get rid of your pain? I always take your pain away, don't I?"

Cindy closed her eyes, half-hoping when she opened them Ben would be gone. But also, half-wishing he would inject her with some drugs to remove the hurt she felt.

Ben looked her in the eyes and spoke in a low, guttural whisper, "I don't have any drugs with me my love."

That statement perplexed her because those were not words that Ben would use.

"I want you to listen to me very carefully. If you follow my instructions, these people will get you somewhere that

I can get drugs for you. The pain you are feeling now will be gone, and I will be there with you, always."

It was hard enough for Cindy to believe that Ben was still alive let alone follow him again into the downward spiral he led her before, but she hurt in every way possible right now. If he could get rid of her sadness, perhaps she should listen.

Ben produced a disposable razor from his coat pocket and held it up for Cindy to see.

"Just break the plastic from around the blades. Remove the blades and use them to make small incisions on your leg. Do you remember the girl you rode with in the jail transport?" Ben quizzed Cindy.

"Yes, I remember her."

"She said she cut herself to ease the pain. When she cut, she felt better. This is the relief I want for you," Ben responded.

At the time it did not occur to Cindy just *how* did Ben know that? He wasn't in the transport van with her. All she did know for sure was she was confused. Nothing made sense then, but she could not resist the temptation to ease her pain. Ben was right, he had always done that for her!

Snapping the plastic that formed the head of the razor Cindy was able to extract two razor blades from the plastic head of the razor. Holding the two blades in her hand she looked up to notice that Ben was gone. Panic almost set in because she didn't know exactly what to do. Then, despite not being able to see Ben, he spoke to her, inside her head.

"Take one of the blades and make a small cut on your leg. It won't hurt," Ben's voice instructed hypnotically, "I promise it will make you feel better!"

With the precision of a surgeon, Cindy began with a small cut. Ben was right, she felt no pain from her flesh being severed. She was intrigued by the crimson liquid as it began to gush from the wound she had created. It was almost like painting a gruesome portrait. Plus, she began to feel better. This was much better than the pain and depression she had felt earlier.

Cindy continued to cut into the side of her left calf. After several more incisions, the cuts sliced deeper, and began to display what appeared to be muscle. This was invigorating to her. Much like the first time she smoked crystal meth at the lake. The deeper she went, the more euphoria she felt.

"Soon, you and I will be where we can be together, forever. I will give you an eternity of pleasure, without pain," Ben's voice echoed as if off of the tall walls of a hollow cathedral.

Cindy smiled at the nurse that entered her room. The nurse screamed in a way that made Cindy wonder why she was acting in such a manner.

"Call an ambulance, urgent, the nurse cried!"

"I never cared for that boy," Demetri thought as he admired the artistry of Cindy's razor work. "Tonight, you came in handy, Pipe, ol' buddy."

The next moment of consciousness that Cindy could recall was waking up in intensive care back at St. Helens Memorial Hospital.

Chapter 22:
Acknowledgement

AS HE STOOD BETWEEN ROOMS 15-1 AND 15-2, Alex felt uneasy. He couldn't understand why he felt this way. It was all the events of the previous day. He couldn't remove the image of the figure he saw in the dining room. That troubled him, and he hoped he would run into the chilling figure again so he could identify who he was, and what he was doing there. He had no viable reason to question this mysterious man, just a feeling.

During their break, Alex asked George Bingham if he might know the man he saw staring at him and Andrea. After all, George saw everybody that came into this hospital.

"Yep, I think he works in the kitchen," George recalled as he sipped his strong coffee. "I don't recall his name right now, but I can find out for you if it's important."

"No, it's not important. I just felt uneasy with him staring at us when I was on my walk with Andrea," Alex replied.

George looked up from his ultra-stained coffee cup with a look of a soldier on high alert. "You gotta trust your instincts, Al. I'll find out who he is. Then maybe we can both feel more comfortable."

Both men shook their heads in affirmation at each other and rose to continue their jobs. George patted Alex on the back and as he exited the break room, he said something that puzzled Alex.

"You have a rare gift that very few humans have," George said.

Before Alex had a chance to quiz George on what he meant by his statement he saw Courtney with her medical cart waving at Alex to let her gain entrance into ward fifteen. Alex waved back at her and smiled as he popped the hydraulic door open so she could gain entrance.

"Hi Alex, miss me?" Courtney laughed.

"Who are you again?" Alex jokingly replied to his crush.

The two passed by rooms one and two and Courtney commented how nice it was that these hadn't been filled lately. Alex smiled and nodded at Courtney, but he was not inclined to share with her that he had a feeling this wouldn't stay this way for long. As they stopped in front of Andrea's room, Courtney asked if Alex could help administer her medications once again.

"I heard that Andrea is a short timer here at ward fifteen," Courtney told Alex, as she prepared the medications.

"That doesn't surprise me. She is doing much better. I'll miss seeing her every day, but since we are in a relationship, I'll just have to make sure to visit her in her new ward," Alex smirked.

Courtney looked at Alex with a puzzled look and responded "Oh, she isn't going to another ward. She is going to be released to go home!"

"Home-home?" Alex replied with a dumbfounded look on his face.

Courtney smiled and said, "Yes, real home. She is going to live with her sister in Vancouver, Washington."

Alex felt both happy and sad at the same time. He felt like he was going to lose a friend with Andrea but in his heart, he knew this day would come. As Alex and Courtney entered her room, Andrea was sitting in the chair by her bed. As usual, she beamed a big smile when she viewed Alex.

"Ah, my boyfriend, come to see me at last," she blushed.

Alex with a sheepish grin scowled at Andrea and said, "Gee, I don't know if we are even together anymore! Rumor has it you are going to leave me and without a word or a note!"

Andrea cackled a huge laugh at Alex's statement. "Well, maybe I have found a new boyfriend in Vancouver!"

"Well, maybe so, but I still love you hippy girl!" Alex acknowledged.

All three laughed as Courtney handed Andrea's medications to Alex. Andrea's face turned somewhat serious for a moment, and she grabbed his hand.

"My dear, you know all too well there are forces inside these walls. You have seen them, and I have seen them," Andrea spoke with a sense of warning.

Alex looked at Andrea and was unable to reply to her revelation.

"The entity that was standing in the dining hall looking at you and I as we finished our courtyard walk the other day, it has been with me for a long time. Ever since my husband died," Andrea stared into Alex's eyes as she spoke with a fervor that made him feel uneasy.

Alex managed to speak despite being confused by what she was saying. "You-you know him?"

"Oh, my dear, I know *it* all too well. It is not a him! His appearance to you and me might be a male, but he is not a human. His purpose is to *deliver* those who do not know the living God! He no longer controls me and that has made him angry. He is afraid of humans like us. Those that can see and speak with them but cannot be controlled because we know the God of Gabriel. He dwells here because he is lazy. This place offers *easy* for him. It offers all that are like him, *easy*," Andrea responded.

Courtney motioned to Alex to continue helping her with her rounds, but it was only to distract him from his conversation and get him out of ear shot from Andrea.

Courtney grabbed Alex by the arm and spoke with a sense of urgency "See, these are the types of things she says that make me concerned that she isn't quite well enough to leave!"

Alex smiled at Courtney and replied, "Trust me, I *know* that Andrea is, and will be safe, when she leaves here!"

Chapter 23:
15-2

TWO WEEKS HAD PASSED and the wounds on Cindy's leg had begun to heal. She had several psychiatric professionals come to see her, and ask various questions about why she felt compelled to hurt herself, and might she do it again? Demetri encouraged her to answer in the affirmative and explain that the first opportunity she had to get something sharp, she would try her wrist!

Her doctors determined that she was well enough to travel and receive evaluation at the Oregon State Mental Hospital in Astoria. Demetri thought this would do just fine. He loved mental hospitals. Those places were *easy*!

A phone call was placed with the administrator at the mental hospital, and it was confirmed that they had two rooms available for criminally charged patients. It was determined that Cindy would be transferred there the day after next. Cindy's doctor had been in contact with her parents about their daughter's progress, and they asked if they could visit her. The doctor determined that no harm could come from a visit with her parents and in fact, it might do her some good. After conferring with the brass at the Sheriff's department, it was confirmed that with a deputy assigned to Cindy, Glen and Margaret could visit.

Glen received the phone call that they had been waiting so long for. He called Margaret at home and told her to pack a bag for both as he was coming home right now to get her, and to drive to St. Helens to see their daughter. Glen prayed as he drove, giving thanks to God for this blessing and asking that nothing get in the way of their visit with Cindy this time. Pulling up into the driveway, Glen barely put the car in park when Margaret appeared out of the front door, toting the bag she had hastily packed.

"I guess she is as excited as I am," Glen thought in amazement.

Glen grabbed the bag and threw it in the trunk of the car as Margaret scurried to the passenger side and climbed in. They discussed what they would say to their daughter during the visit and decided the best thing would be to just show her they loved her, supported her, and would do anything they could to help get her better. They both knew it would be an uphill battle, but with God behind them, nothing was impossible.

Demetri felt uneasy about the visit his subject was about to receive, and he didn't know how to stop it this time. He determined he had her deep in his control appearing to her as Ben, and there wasn't much her parents could say or do to stop him. He just hated to think he would have to endure hearing how wonderful their God was, and why she should surrender to him. *His* master was more powerful, and he had been endowed with that power, so why not bring it on. He was up for a challenge. Perhaps that was why he had become so bored. He needed this challenge.

"Yes-yes, bring it on!" Demetri smiled.

An ambulance pulled up to a private entrance at Mariners Hospital to transport Cindy to her new residence at the State Mental Hospital in Astoria. Her doctor came to speak with her one last time to reassure her this was the best situation for her. In Astoria they could provide around the clock care, and counseling, to help her deal with her depression and hopefully get her feeling better. Cindy listened but didn't really understand how this could make her feel better. She already learned how to do that with Ben's help, and a sharp instrument.

Cindy was strapped down onto a gurney and loaded into an ambulance for the journey. She noticed she had a new deputy escorting her for this trip. The deputy introduced herself as Deputy Martinez who would be with her all the way to Astoria. Cindy inquired if she would be attending her all the time now. This deputy had kind, big brown eyes. Martinez had short cut hair, but you would never mistake that she was a woman. Even through a bullet-proof vest and the classic uniform, Cindy admired her and was just slightly jealous that such a strong woman could also reveal a soft side.

"No, just for this trip. Once we get you settled in Astoria you will be getting somebody from the Astoria PD," Martinez answered.

Demetri was glad that this officer would not be with them. Her kind soul probably meant she was a believer in Gabriel's God, and he had seen enough of *those* people lately.

The trip went uneventful. The ambulance pulled into the intake garage at Astoria and came to a stop. Cindy's anxiety was high, and she hoped that the staff here would be friendly and helpful. As the back doors of the ambulance flew open Cindy could see several people attending to her gurney and removing her from the ambulance. Everybody that was attending to her appeared to be medical staff, because they were all in medical scrubs of assorted colors and patterns. Cindy wished she could have a pair of scrubs just like them.

The gurney moved swiftly down a hallway, but based on the way she was strapped in, all Cindy could see were the overhead lights in the ceiling. She marveled at how white everything seemed. From the walls to the ceiling. She was glad the nursing staff wore such brightly colored scrubs otherwise everybody might just disappear into the surroundings. Cindy finally came to stop at a doorway that a short minute later slid to an open position. The staff pushed her gurney through that doorway, and into another.

As she rolled through the second doorway, she could see painted over the top of the door were the numbers 15-2.

Chapter 24:
Settling In

IT HAD BEEN A LONG TIME since room 2 in Ward 15 had seen an occupant. Alex had been disturbed by his sense of perception that one or both of the inmate rooms would be filled again. His perceptions and intuition were coming true. He stood in the hallway outside room two waiting for the doctor and nursing staff to come out of the room and brief them on their new patient, Cindy Firestone. Courtney joined Alex in the hallway and affirmed they would be briefed soon.

She smiled at Alex and said, "She is a very young girl. Pretty eyes and very thin."

The charge nurse and doctor came out into the hallway and shut the door to room two. The doctor held Cindy's chart and after gaining everybody's attention spoke "The patient is twenty years old and suffering from a chemical dependency on methamphetamines, heroin, and cocaine. Diagnosis reports from Mariner's are she suffers from schizophrenia, bi-polar disorder, and self- inflicted wounds or *cutting.*" The doctor looked at Alex directly like a kid that had been caught misbehaving and said "She hasn't shown any violent tendencies so far, Alex, and her charges aren't violent in nature, but I would still be incredibly careful with her. She will have a twenty-four-hour police escort while she is in our care, so make sure that escort accompanies you wherever you go with her."

"Copy that, doc," Alex replied.

With Alex and Courtney up to speed on their day-to-day chores of caring for Ms. Firestone, the staff broke up and scurried off to see other patients. Alex and Courtney looked at each other and simultaneously let out big sighs and headed into Cindy's room for the meet and greet with their new patient. Cindy appeared almost asleep as Alex and Courtney approached her bed. Alex decided he would go first and introduced himself.

"Hello Ms. Firestone, my name is Alex Dante. My responsibility is to assist you with anything you might need. If you need to go anywhere in this hospital, I will be the person to get you there. Well, that is except for the bathroom. Officer Johnson here will have to help you with that because she is the boss when it comes to you!"

Officer Johnson was a Black, female officer. She was tall and muscular, and Alex would not want to tangle with her.

She replied to Alex's statement "He knows the routine Ms. Firestone. You need those restraints to come off, I got to be the one to do it!"

Cindy didn't smile but acknowledged what Alex and Officer Johnson just told her.

Alex continued "This is Nurse Courtney. We are usually on shift together so if you need anything medical in nature, just ask for me and I will call for Courtney."

With that introduction Courtney formally introduced herself to Cindy and explained she would be giving her medications, as prescribed, twice a day. Once in the morning, and once at supper time. She would also be checking the wounds on her leg.

Courtney proceeded to unwrap the bandages on Cindy's legs and although she had been nursing for almost ten years, she couldn't imagine how somebody could have self-inflicted those wounds and not passed out. She changed Cindy's bandages and wrapped them again, smiled at her new patient, and told her she would be back later to check on her. Alex followed Courtney out of room two, but before departing asked Officer Johnson if she needed anything.

"No sir, I appreciate you asking but I'm good," Officer Johnson smiled at Alex.

Alex closed the door behind them, and Courtney said, "Poor kid, I hope they can find a way to help her. She seems so lost in so many ways."

Alex replied, "I am sure glad I have you here to help me buddy."

Courtney started a broad smile directed towards Alex and in a questioning manner asked him, "So, I'm off this Friday, Saturday and Sunday. Any chance our days off coincide so you can take me to Saturday Market in Portland?"

Alex felt he would have called in sick if he didn't already have those days off. "Pick you up at your place at 8:30 AM on Saturday!"

Courtney and Alex's joint smiles could have lit a dark cave in the Amazon rainforest the rest of the day.

Later that afternoon Officer Johnson peered up from her book she was reading to view Cindy talking to herself. She could tell Cindy was asleep and shrugged it off as normal. While she was asleep from the activities of the day Cindy heard Benjamin speak to her.

"Good job my love. Now we are in a place where I can work to bring you peace and comfort."

Cindy mumbled, "But Pipe, I don't know if I want the drugs anymore. I like the way the cutting made me feel.

Can't I just do that? I just do not want to get in any more trouble. I'm already in so much trouble."

Although Cindy could not see Ben like before she could hear him in her head loud and clear.

"Don't fret my love. It is not drugs or cutting I will give you. You will be with me soon, and I will love you forever."

Chapter 25:
Visitation

THE RAIN CONTINUED TO FALL IN ASTORIA as Glen and Margaret Firestone pulled into a parking spot designated for visitors at the Hospital. They were both feeling a great deal of anxiety due to the previously attempted visit with their daughter having failed. Putting the transmission into park, Glen shut off the engine and looked over to Margaret. "Here we go again, Mag." They exited the car together when Glen stopped and glanced back into the car. "I forgot the bible. Should we try and take it in? Do you think they will let us give it to her?" Glen quizzed.

Margaret answered "Yes, take it with us. The worst they can say is *no*."

Glen grabbed the bible from the car, shut the door again and together he and his wife walked towards the entrance of the hospital. Opening the door to the entrance Glen and Margaret were greeted by a short, stocky man in a black polo shirt adorned with the words *SECURITY* in white on the back of his shirt. His name tag on the front of the shirt said George Bingham.

"Hi folks, how can I help you?" George inquired.

Glen responded, "We are Glen and Margaret Firestone, here to visit Cynthia Firestone."

"Ah yes, the Firestones. Since this is your first visit with us folks, I'll give you the lay of the land, so you know what to expect," George replied.

"We greatly appreciate that Mr. Bingham. It has been several months since we have seen our daughter. We are quite nervous," Glen offered.

"Happy to help Mr. Firestone. First, since your daughter is with us facing criminal charges, your visit with her will be behind glass today. Unfortunately, there will only be one phone receiver on your side of the glass, and one phone receiver on your daughters' side. So only you, or your wife, will be able to talk and hear your daughter at a time. Sorry, but that is the only way you can visit with her for now," George explained.

Glen in earnest replied, "This way will be a blessing for us."

"Good, some folks get a little upset that these visits aren't in person, and I just didn't want you to be surprised," George continued.

"How about the bible Mr. Bingham. Can she get the bible?" Glen quizzed.

George held the bible in his hand and shuffled through the pages in inspection. "I will submit it to her doctor and if he approves for her to get it, then I will make sure she receives it."

"Thank you, Mr. Bingham," Glen smiled.

"I'm going to buzz you through into the main hospital," George instructed. "After you pass through this main door, the visiting center will be clearly marked on your left. You and Mrs. Firestone can take a seat in visiting booth number two. I can't promise how quick they can get Cynthia there, but they will go as quickly as they can."

Glen and Margaret passed by George and as they went through the main door towards the visit area, Glen glanced back at George and smiled. George began to close the door behind them and called out "Have a blessed visit Pastor."

They found visit booth two and opened the door. The seating was vinyl 1950's but neither cared about the comfort of the seating arrangements. Glen helped Margaret remove her jacket and once she had positioned herself in her respective chair, he closed his eyes and said a quick prayer. The content of his prayer he left up to Jesus. As he waited for his daughter to arrive on the other side of the glass something odd occurred to Glen.

He never mentioned to George that he was a Pastor.

Chapter 26:
Safety

OPENING THE DOOR TO ROOM NUMBER TWO very slowly, Alex peeked in and caught the eye of Officer Johnson. He noticed that Cindy was sleeping and as much as he did not want to disturb her much needed rest, he calculated just how important the news he was bringing to her.

"Officer Johnson, Ms. Firestone's doctor cleared her for visitors, and she has one waiting for her," Alex said in a whisper. He was startled after whispering the news to Officer Johnson that Cindy's eyes suddenly popped wide open.

"Is – is it my Mom and Dad?" Cindy asked in a strained tone.

"Yes, I believe it is," Alex answered.

Cindy began to struggle against the restraints in an excited manner.

"Whoa there girl!" Johnson called out, "Do you want to visit with your folks, Ms. Firestone?"

Cindy nodded and replied, "Please, more than anything!"

Officer Johnson explained to Cindy that she would remove the restraints around her feet and one arm so that Alex could help her into a wheelchair. She also gave Cindy chapter and verse that if she tried anything during her transfer to the wheelchair that Cindy would get to experience the joy of being *tased*. Cindy offered that she would be no trouble at all because the last thing she wanted was to jeopardize this visit with her Mom and Dad.

With the restraints removed, Alex told Cindy to put her left arm around his neck and he would gently swing her legs, along with her torso to a sitting position on her bed. He went as slow as possible due to the fear her leg wounds must hurt, but she never flinched during her transfer from her bed to the wheelchair.

With the impending visit, Demetri wasn't quite sure what this new sensation was that he was feeling. It started when Cindy reached her arm over Alex's shoulder and grasped his neck. What was this sensation? He had never felt this before, so he had no reference point in his past to acquaint himself with. "This is quite discerning to be feeling this, at this time. He needed to be in control. Complete control," Demetri thought.

Then it occurred to him, he might know what this feeling was. It might be fear. Just as soon as the feeling came, it went away, just at the same time she let go of Alex.

Alex was amazed just how smooth Cindy managed the transition from her bed into the wheelchair. The threesome of Alex, Cindy and Officer Johnson wheeled out of room two and ward fifteen into the hallway that would take them to the secured side of the visiting booths. As they traveled the route that would reunite her with her parents, Cindy knew nothing would get in the way today. No seizure, no Benjamin, no Pipeline, no drugs. When she put her arm around Alex's neck, she felt something she had not felt in months. She felt safe, and strong. Alex came to visit booth number two and ran his magnetic card on the electronic lock to open it up.

As Cindy rolled through the door she looked up at Alex and smiled with closed lips as she didn't want him to see her missing tooth.

"This will not do! Not at all!" Dimitri pouted, "Whoever this human is, he has disturbed me. I must learn more about why. It is much too late in the game to lose control!"

Chapter 27:
Reunion

THE APPEARANCE OF THEIR DAUGHTER WAS A SHOCK. She was much thinner than Margaret could have imagined. Still, it was Cindy, and after so many months separated it didn't matter how sick she appeared. Glen wished he could transport through the glass and pick her up in his arms and never let her go. As hard as it was for him, to not just grab the phone and bellow his happiness all over the receiver, his better sense of gentlemanly decorum came over him and he told Margaret to go first.

Cindy was trembling as she picked up the receiver on her side. None of the three Firestones had a dry eye. She held the receiver to her ear and spoke, 'Mommy, it is so good to see you and Daddy. I am so sorry – so sorry – so....' And with that her trembling and tears turned into heavy sobs as she laid the receiver down.

Alex or Officer Johnson weren't required to be in the visiting booth with Cindy because it wasn't a contact visit, but Alex could see she was overcome with emotion. He scanned his card on his side and entered behind Cindy's wheelchair. He reached around Cindy and picked up the receiver and spoke to Margaret Firestone. "Mrs. Firestone, my name is Alex Dante. I am a caregiver for your daughter while she is staying with us. If you will give Cindy just a moment, I'm sure she will be all right to talk to you."

Margaret watched Alex through tear-stained eyes as he spoke to her. A warmth fell over her and she wasn't sure why or how, but she felt like with this man caring for her daughter, she would be fine.

"Thank you so much Alex, Bless you. Our daughter's name is Cindy. Please call her Cindy," Margaret cried.

Alex came around to Cindy's side and got down on one knee to be at eye level with her. "Cindy, take your time. Cry it out if you want to. Your mother and father are here because they love you and miss you. Just to see your face is enough for them," Alex spoke with a tenderness and compassion Cindy hadn't heard in a long, long time. His words were sincere and believable, unlike those of Ben Tasker.

Picking up the phone receiver with the newfound composure she received from Alex, her direction turned back towards her mother, and she said, "Hi, Mommy. I have missed you. Are you taking good care of Daddy?"

Margaret replied, "Of course sweetheart. Who else could take care of your father except me?"

Mother and daughter found their new tears were now from laughter. The girls continued to talk and although Glen could not hear what Cindy was saying he was immensely proud at how Margaret's end of the conversation was not as a controlling mother, but as a friend. Knowing that their visit couldn't last forever, Cindy asked her Mother if she should speak with her Dad. Margaret ended her conversation with, "I love you baby. You will always be my baby." Then Margaret handed the phone to Glen.

Knowing that her father was the levelheaded, practical one in the family, Cindy shared the same conversation with Glen as she had with her Mom but was more inquisitive as to the legal issues that faced her. He felt it was best to be honest with Cindy as he had always practiced what he preached. Glen let Cindy know that her charges were extensive and serious but all of that was on hold until they evaluated her mental state.

"I suppose that makes sense based on everything that I have done to myself," Cindy solemnly conceded.

"Honey, the best thing we can do for you now is to help you get better. Do what they say, and take all the help they offer here," Glen implored.

Cindy nodded in favor of what her Father had just told her when a voice came over the phone telling both parties that their visit would end in one minute. Cindy thanked her parents for coming and knew in her heart she would get better and be with them again soon. Glen agreed. Then Cindy asked one last question of her father knowing that their communication would soon end but she also knew glass could not separate this request from each other.

"Dad, can you pray for me?" Cindy asked with her last words.

The entire visit had been a bit uneventful for Demetri. He had begun to wonder what all the fuss was about, and why he was concerned, to have Cindy face this human man of God she called father. He had been lulled into a false sense of security in his control of Cindy. Too many things had happened today with this encounter with the human Alex, and now this request coming from her. He felt sucker punched and livid that she would even ask that question. The God of Gabriel could do nothing now to help her, and Demetri decided he must act quickly, much more quickly than he had originally planned.

When Glen and Margaret entered the portal to exit the hospital, Glen had hoped to see the guard that knew he was a pastor. George wasn't there and Glen hoped to remember to ask him on their next visit. As the Firestones settled in their car to drive to the hotel Glen looked at Margaret and spoke.

"I know we have never met Cindy's attendant but just watching him speak to our daughter, I sensed something special about him. I'm not sure what it is, just something special."

Margaret replied to Glen's statement, "That makes two of us. A mother's intuition maybe, but I just felt-uh-there was something different about him. It was a feeling of comfort."

They drove to the hotel, both deep in thought but satisfaction that God had begun to heal their daughter, and even them.

Chapter 28:
Old Acquaintances

THE HOSPITAL HAD MOVED BEYOND THE ACTIVITY of the day and settled into the calm that the nighttime brings to staff and patients alike. Cindy had retired to slumber but Demetri was restless. He had been challenged before, but nothing like this. His sense of having Cindy deeply in his control and moving toward delivery of her soul was now in jeopardy. He abandoned his indwelling of Cindy and her current state of rest, to walk alone for a short time. He needed to get away from mortals. At least *these* mortals.

Demetri glanced around room number two and at the human that had relieved Officer Johnson. This mortal seemed younger in human age. Perhaps the fact she had less life experience would prove to be beneficial to him later. If he could utilize her youth to his advantage, he certainly must. He must come up with a plan, and soon. As much as Cindy intrigued him, almost as much as the woman from 1920, he had underestimated her. He often thought he got a little too impatient in 1920 and let her go too soon. Demetri hoped he wasn't making the same mistake with Cindy Firestone.

The breakroom in ward fifteen proved to be a good spot for Demetri to sit, reflect and plan his next move. The rain had subsided for a moment and the clouds had broken up in the Oregon sky just enough to allow moonlight to peek through the barred window and cast a dim light on the breakroom. As he sat in the white resin chair, he wondered why humans even bothered to have a chair like this, but it was all there was, and it would have to make do.

Demetri closed his demon eyes and caught a glimpse in his memory of his past. He saw his woman from 1920. Tall, slender, blonde bobbed hair with a black amulet broach across her forehead acting like a headband. Her high cheekbones accented her smile with ruby lips. He could not recall a more beautiful human. That was why he let her go so quickly. He desired to be human because of her. Demetri let out a pained laugh. Throwing his golden hair back he ran his fingers through it to make it go into place to form a braid. Then he heard a grunt of amusement. An annoying sound that was all too recognizable. Demetri had not heard that sound in several hundred years and he could have tolerated not hearing it for several hundred more.

Standing before him looking up at the moon glow coming through the window was his fellow demon, Gayland.

"Well, Demetri, my dearest friend," Gayland smirked as he continued to stare out the window. "I thought this place was beneath your dignity," he continued as he turned to face Demetri.

Had Demetri known that Gayland was here, he would have thought twice about accepting this as the place to ponder his work on capturing Cindy's soul.

"Oh, now that I know you are here Gayland, it makes me even more excited this is where I have arrived. How proud the master must be of you for all your hard effort," Demetri replied with all the sarcasm he could muster.

Gayland would only dignify that remark with the slightest of smiles. He pulled up another white resin chair and using it to straddle his torso to the back of the chair he faced Demetri, "Mock me as you may my dear Demetri, but I have delivered many more souls to our master at this place than you have gallivanting around the planet. Our master cannot deny the numbers I have provided."

Despite wanting to continue the sarcastic duel with Gayland, Demetri knew that in a way this lazy demon was right. Mental hospitals were rich with opportunities to serve their master and this was the reason he chose this place for Cindy. He wondered if much like Gayland, *he* had grown lazy.

"It appears that this girl has presented some trouble for the mighty Demetri. You might mock me for conducting my business here in this place but as you will find out, there are adversaries in this place that could cause you to lose this one," Gayland said straight faced.

Knocking his chair back into a corner of the room, Demetri sprang from it and grabbed Gayland by the collar of his precious black leather jacket. Holding Gayland against the white cinder block wall by the collar, Gayland studied the anger in Demetri's face.

Demetri growled as an angry lion with assurance, "Listen angel, you don't have one ounce of my ability. Our master knows it, and you know it. I have not lost this one by any means. I am **Demetri!** The deliverer of souls and this girl with the blind eyes will not defeat me, ever!"

Gayland knew he was no match for Demetri. It would be folly to try. He also knew that what Demetri said was very true. He could not come close to the favor that Demetri had with their master. Still, his jealousy could not be quenched by just backing down.

Gayland began his departure from Demetri knowing he had struck a chord of doubt in his mind. With one last opportunity to throw a punch and face no retaliation,

Gayland quipped at Demetri who had released him and begun to calm down.

"Not that you need my advice mighty demon, but I certainly know your current subject can't defeat you! It is not the girl with the special eyes you need to worry about. It is not even her father who worships Gabriel's God. Your worry and your challenge come from the human that attends to her. The human they call Alex!"

Chapter 29:
A Departing

AFTER HAVING A NIGHT OF FITFUL SLEEP, deep in odd dreams and with an inability to get comfortable, Alex turned his fatigue towards thoughts of Courtney. This would be his last day of work for three days and with those days off would come his first date with the girl of his dreams. He had to focus on his upcoming trip to Saturday Market in Portland, or today would be difficult to survive.

Alex incoherently walked through most of the normal activity of getting ready for work and trudged out to his car. He was grateful that today he did not find any drug paraphernalia and after inserting his belongings into the seat beside him, he turned the engine over and began the drive to the hospital. He enjoyed listening to KLUV-107 Christian radio as he drove to and from work when various pastors played some of their recent sermons. He had his favorite radio pastors, and joked to himself, it was like going to church while driving.

The pastor that was giving his sermon on this drive was one that Alex hadn't heard before. He must be new to this station, he thought, but he enjoyed his tone, and the content of his sermon was quite interesting. The pastor spoke on the existence of angels and what they are. Of course, in his explanation of angels he validated the existence of demons. He went on to explain we are caught up in a battle of light and dark and spiritual warfare was very real. As Alex turned into the parking lot of the hospital, he wished he could spare another ten minutes to finish this program but the work clock was ticking and he knew he must hurry into his post. "Maybe I can find this sermon on a podcast later," he thought to himself.

Alex scurried past George as he tapped the coffee thermos to show him that he brought an ample supply for George to share. George winked his approval back towards Alex as he moved quickly down the hallway to the entrance of Ward 15. Inserting his key card into the electronic reader, the door to Ward 15 opened. Alex received quite a shock to see his supervisor, Amy Hess standing there waiting for him. His first thoughts were that he was in trouble, once again for being late, but the clock on the wall showed he still had one minute to spare.

"Hey boss, long time no see, which I believe is a good thing, right?" Alex quizzed Amy.

"That is true Mr. Dante, but don't fret about my appearance today. I'm actually here to ask you for a favor."

"Sure, anything Amy. What can I do?"

Alex professing the word "anything" left him wide open to get trapped into agreeing to something he would soon regret.

With a look of disgust Amy responded, "Well, your graveyard counterpart that you share Ward 15 with has decided to suddenly leave us. Apparently, your *friend* in room 2 only responds well to you Mr. Dante."

"Jesse is gone. I have worked with him in this ward for years. We knew how each other worked without even sharing information. It seems so odd that Ms. Firestone could cause him to quit?" Alex said in a puzzled fashion.

"Well, she did. Alex, I need you to hang in there for me until I can get somebody who can work with these difficult patients, like you can. Unfortunately, I need you to work overtime through your days off. I know you're tired, but these patients are very sensitive to change, and you are all they know. You are their *rock*," Amy smiled.

Alex stared down at the linoleum floor pondering what his supervisor had just asked of him. He felt his date with Courtney slipping away. He knew in all reality she wasn't asking just anything. He really had no choice. "A single rock is more like it," Alex responded.

"I'm sorry, I didn't catch what you just said?" Amy quizzed.

Alex answered in a voice that was audible "I'll be here, boss."

"Thank you, Alex. You are much appreciated, and I owe you for this," she echoed as she scanned her card to exit ward fifteen.

Alex answered as she left ear shot, "Maybe owe should mean a raise, or I might just follow Jesse out the door," he grumbled.

Despite it being very difficult to focus on the work at hand, Alex was a professional and realized he must concentrate on his patients. He wasn't sure how, or even *if,* Cindy Firestone could have caused his co-worker's departure, but he couldn't hold it against her. This poor girl had been through enough and did not deserve any wrath from him. Alex put on his best face and tapped on the door to room number two. Officer Johnson motioned for Alex to enter the room.

Cindy was restrained to the hospital bed, but her head was elevated to almost a sitting position. She was watching television when her head turned to face Alex as he entered the room.

"Ms. Firestone, good morning," Alex said.

In a scratchy voice Cindy returned the greeting. "Hi," she bashfully said. "Can you call me Cindy? Like is it allowed?"

Officer Johnson chimed into her question, "No girl, callin you by your first name is a second-class misdemeanor." Moving from the straight face that answered that question, Johnson broke into a jovial laugh. "Just kidding girl, he can call you whatever he wants!"

Cindy and Alex both joined in with laughs to Officer Johnson's comment. Alex explained to Cindy that she was scheduled to meet with Dr. Rosen, the hospital psychiatrist, at 10:00 AM in his office and she should start getting ready for him, and Officer Johnson, to transport her. He told her it was about a ten-minute trip. Looking at the clock Cindy and Officer Johnson realized she had about thirty minutes to get ready. Alex acknowledged with her that he would return in thirty to get Cindy and left the girls to their privacy.

Courtney was standing outside of Cindy's room when Alex appeared. At first her smile was directed at seeing Alex, but then her look became a bit somber. She reluctantly spoke, "Hey, uhm, I think you're going to be upset with me Alex."

"Why would I be upset with you?" Alex responded with a confused look.

"I just found out I have to work this weekend. So that means our trip to the Saturday Market is off," Courtney replied with utter disappointment.

In a laugh remarkably similar to the one Officer Johnson just had, Alex let out a bellow of his own. He honestly didn't know if he should be sad or relieved by Courtney's revelation.

"Why are you laughing at me Mr. Dante?" Courtney asked with indignation.

"I'm not laughing at you! I am laughing because Amy Hess just told me that I have to work also. I wasn't sure how I was going to tell you because, frankly, it was the only thing I have looked forward to in months. I thought *you* would be mad at *me!*" Alex confessed.

Courtney looked around the hallway to make sure there was nobody around to see them. She moved closer to Alex, placed both her hands on his broad shoulders and gave him a quick kiss on his lips.

"That will have to keep you Mr. Dante until we can have our real date," Courtney seductively offered to Alex.

"Oh, that will keep me all right. That will more than suffice to keep me," Alex gushed.

Alex pressed his fingertips to his freshly kissed lips, as if to lock the memory of it like a trophy in a glass case.

Courtney proceeded into the room of Cindy Firestone and Alex moved on to see his Hippy Girl, Andrea Best. Alex knocked on her door and announced he was there to check on her. Andrea called for Alex to enter her room in Ward 15 and upon doing so, he was shocked to see Andrea fully dressed and all her belongings packed.

"Andrea, I wasn't notified you were getting discharged today."

"It was sudden, my dear Alex. My sister and her husband were anxious to get me home, and frankly I was as anxious as they were. Dr. Rosen decided there was really no reason for me to stay here any longer. My meds were controlled and at the right dosage, so off I go when my sis gets here to pick me up," Andrea confessed.

Alex was a bit saddened by the fact he was losing his friend. He knew it would not be the same without her. As happy as he was for Andrea, questioned the logic of her mental health being normal!

"Andrea, does Dr. Rosen know you still see, you know, *things*?" Alex asked in the most sensitive manner he could imagine. With that question thrown out towards her,

Alex noticed that Andrea's rosary wasn't in her hand. He knew that rosary was never far from her possession.

Andrea very carefully replied, "Alex, does Dr. Rosen know *you* see things? What we both see is the same thing. It is not human and is spawned of evil. Dr. Rosen and all his medications will not help what we see because it is not in our minds, it is real."

"I noticed you don't have your husband's rosary with you Andrea?" Alex quizzed.

"I no longer pray for my husband. He is with the true and living God now. His rosary will not save or protect me, or you dear Alex. Much like you, I belong to the living God. The demon that had me until Jesus set me free is named Gayland. He fears me now and has left me. More than his fear of me, he fears you even more. That is why he gazed upon you. He knew you are a different type of human," Andrea shared with Alex.

He sat and stared into Andrea's face with astonishment in her revelation that the existence of demons was real and present.

Alex hugged Andrea and gave her a kiss on the cheek. This was the most Godly, strong woman he had ever known and somehow, he feared this might be the last time he saw her on earth.

Chapter 30:
Tick Tock

EACH DAY ALEX WOULD PUSH CINDY FIRESTONE in her wheelchair to Dr. Rosen's office, and just like all the patients that came into the care of Alex Dante at the State Mental Hospital, she felt comfort and security with him. Cindy felt enough comfort with Alex that she began to share all the elements of her life with him. Despite making him feel a little uncomfortable, Alex listened and commented on things he felt were appropriate to do so.

He wondered how Officer Johnson viewed these conversations. Was she curious why Cindy shared more of her life with Alex than Dr. Rosen? Alex had to quit letting his mind wander into wondering these things, and just accept that this young woman wanted and needed his attention.

Since the ten-minute trips to and from Dr. Rosen's office didn't seem to be sufficient for Cindy, she asked the doctor for permission, on nice days, which in Astoria meant days without rain, for Alex to escort her into the courtyard. Dr. Rosen felt that these excursions could be beneficial for Cindy, both to share in some normal human interaction, and since her wounds had significantly healed, plus to get a degree of exercise and physical therapy.

Dr. Rosen consulted with Amy Hess who agreed to add this to Alex's daily schedule with the permission of Cindy's law enforcement escort. Officer Johnson showed no resistance to the idea since it seemed that Cindy showed a calmer demeanor when around Alex. The fits of talking in her sleep and just staring at nothing seemed to lessen when Alex was around. Perhaps Cindy was smitten with Alex, she thought, and who wouldn't be. Alex Dante was a good-looking man, the officer thought. She just hoped that Cindy would not go too far down that rabbit hole, because as a woman, Johnson had witnessed how Alex acted around Nurse Courtney. The boy certainly had a *thing* for her, and that could break a young girl's heart.

When Alex was told he would start taking Cindy on short walks in the courtyard he didn't seem to object. He missed his time outside with Andrea Best, now that she was gone, and he enjoyed getting to know this troubled girl.

Each day that Alex was now in Cindy's life was a difficult day for Demetri. He was not amused by his methods and what disturbed him the most is when Cindy was with Alex, he felt like *he* wasn't in control. His resolve to end this habitation was becoming ever so clear. He didn't want it to end but feared this would be just like the woman from 1920, he would have to let her go too soon. Demetri was certain that episode had caused a void in his existence, and he vowed he would not let Cindy go too soon. That thought seemed to be vanishing now that Alex Dante was in the picture.

By the labor laws of the state of Oregon, Alex had to have a day off. He was exhausted and despite his desire to have his day off, he knew it would not be enough to get any rest. When Alex did sleep, it was restless, and this had begun to worry him. The events of ward fifteen, with the arrival of Cindy Firestone, and the revelation from Andrea that he had witnessed seeing a demon, had obviously taken their toll on Alex.

After his day off, Alex walked into the start of his shift in ward fifteen and peeked in on Officer Johnson and Cindy. The officer was elated to see Alex and said, "Whoo boy, no more days off for you! Our girl was quite restless in your absence. I'm not sure who she was talking with, but it certainly wasn't me!"

Cindy, upon seeing Alex smiled broadly and spoke, "Hello Alex. Glad your back."

Alex reciprocated her smile although he was bothered to hear she struggled with reality when he was not there. The more that occurred, the less opportunity he had to get some time away from the hospital and he desperately wanted to embark on a deeper relationship with Courtney.

"Hey, I have a surprise for you Ms. Cynthia," Alex called out to her.

Cindy eagerly responded, "You do? What is it?"

"How about a short walk outside in the courtyard. We can take your wheelchair just in case you get tired," Alex quizzed.

She anxiously replied, "You will-can do that for me?"

"Yep, just for you," he responded.

Alex explained he would give her and Officer Johnson a few minutes to get ready as he would make his rounds to see his other patients.

Demetri fretted. The previous day had gone so well without Alex present. Benjamin Tasker had come to visit and was quite convincing in his argument that he, and only he, loved Cindy and she must place her allegiance in him. Demetri had learned from this foe and displayed all the patience and kindness that Alex had shown to Cindy. Demetri thought "If you can't beat them, join them!" Still, despite feeling he had made inroads into controlling Cindy again, it paled in comparison to when Alex walked into the room. Now with Alex escorting her today, he once again would feel powerless to confront this human.

Alex returned to room two to begin his time with Cindy. Helping her into her wheelchair he explained she could get up and walk with him just as soon as they got outside into the courtyard. Alex noticed that Cindy had put on a small amount of eye shadow and liner. It must have been with the help and approval of Johnson. Alex thought it would have been rude and counter-productive to Cindy's recovery if he didn't say something to her.

"I must say Cindy, you look very nice today. Obviously trips to the courtyard agree with you," Alex mused.

Looking back at Officer Johnson, he could see she was looking down at the pathway but had a smile on her face. Cindy would not try to hide her smile. It was broad and beaming and showed no embarrassment for her missing tooth. After a short time of quiet which the threesome all appeared to be enjoying, Cindy spoke to break the silence.

"Did you know I am a PK?" Cindy asked.

"A PK?" Alex said in a puzzled fashion.

"A Pastor's kid," Cindy answered.

"No-no I didn't know that," Alex responded.

"My father is Pastor of Seaside Community Church. He started the church just before I was born. It has thrived and grown to the largest church on the coast of Oregon. Unfortunately, I didn't grow and thrive like the church," Cindy expounded.

Alex was a bit stumped on how to reply to her statement. He opted that at this early stage of their relationship it was best to not answer her. If Alex had been stumped by Cindy's last statement it paled in comparison to her next question directed towards him.

"How many times have you made love, Alex? It doesn't have to be an exact number, just your best guess?"

He was stupefied by her question. This was a direct question she had asked him and the one thing he had been taught was to not ignore or lie to a patient when they ask you a question. He thought he could just tell her he preferred not to answer her question, or he could reprimand her for asking a personal question, but Alex decided for better or worse he would just answer it honestly.

"Cindy, I am a virgin. No joke. I am saving my first time for my bride who I marry," Alex responded with all seriousness.

Alex couldn't help but look at the response on Johnson's face which was one of surprise.

"Then you must be a believer in Jesus," Cindy replied.

Alex knew that discussions on beliefs and religion were forbidden with patients, and this statement from Cindy had all the earmark of trouble for him if he answered. He noticed that Cindy's walk had begun to slow quite a bit and thought this might be his opportunity to escape this conversation.

"Are you getting tired Cindy? Would you lie to sit down?" Alex inquired.

Cindy expressed her desire to sit on the same bench he had shared with Andrea during one of their walks. Glancing up towards the dining room he was relieved to see nobody standing there looking at them this time.

"I myself, have had sex," Cindy said as if confessing to a Priest.

Alex had hoped this conversation would go away but he was mistaken.

"I have never made love though. What I thought was love, really wasn't. The only man I have had sex with was Ben. He did not know how to make love. He only cared about his pleasure, not mine," she said.

"Yes, some men are like that Cindy," Alex responded.

"Then why does he tell me he loves me now?" Cindy asked.

Chapter 31:
Phone Call

WITH THE SUN SETTING ON THE WESTERN HORIZON, Alex sat in a folding lawn chair admiring the hues of red and orange forming a silhouette against the few clouds that existed. It was rare that the weather provided the opportunity for him to sit out on his small and meager porch at his home. He was enjoying a cold can of cherry soda when the microwave gave its ding of completion that his frozen dinner was ready.

He didn't eat, or like frozen dinners, but he was too exhausted to cook tonight, and he couldn't shake the recent conversation he had with Cindy Firestone out of his mind. He pulled the remaining plastic covering off the mashed potatoes and Salisbury steak dinner that he had so expertly prepared with all the culinary skill he could manage. It didn't take long to consume the meager portions of this meal, and he decided that the disappearance of the seagulls scavenging for their evening supper meant it was time to go inside for the night.

He clicked on his television, which by today's standards would be considered an antique, but he felt no need to purchase a TV based on how often he watched it. Alex preferred to read or listen to Christian radio. He was on his third read through the bible, and would pick up bible studies whenever a subject, usually one a radio pastor had preached on, interested him. He thought he must go to the local bible bookstore and get a study or some literature on Angels and Demons. Tonight, held no intellectual opportunity for Alex. He sensed turning on the TV would provide a short distraction before he would fall asleep.

He laid on his bumpy old couch and propped his head up with a pillow that had also seen better days. Void of getting sucked into the technology age, Alex's source of phone calls was an old-fashioned landline telephone. Just as he had reached a comfort level on the couch the phone rang. He seldom received calls at home, so he was slightly startled. Picking up the receiver Alex propositioned the caller on the other end with some basic humor, "hello, thanks for calling Alex's house of culinary delights."

The voice on the other end was silent for a few moments before speaking.

"Alex, is that you?"

He recognized immediately that it was Courtney. His heart began to pump faster, and he scrambled to sit up to be more attentive to her call.

"I didn't get to see you before you left work today and just wanted to say hi, and goodnight," She spoke in a soft and seductive manner.

Two hours later the phone call ended, and Alex threw one arm over his forehead and thought to himself, "this is the girl that will be my first, and as Cindy Firestone longed to understand, she will be my wife and on our wedding night, *we* will make love."

Chapter 32:
A Battle

DR. ROSEN FINISHED THE PHONE CALL and hung up with Glen Firestone. It was not a promising diagnosis that Cindy would be well, anytime soon. At this juncture of her therapy, he advised Glen and Margaret that he was going to submit his findings to the St. Helen's District Attorney that Cynthia was unfit to stand trial and couldn't understand the charges against her. Dr. Rosen said the good news is Cindy could avoid all the criminal proceedings and possible prison time based on his diagnosis. But the bad news is, she could face many more years in the State Mental Hospital. Glen bowed his head after ending the call. This time not to pray, but to cry.

In the darkness of room two, Benjamin sat on Cindy's bed and created the illusion in her mind he was stroking her hair.

"I understand why you're so confused about my desire for your body and my impatience with you not feeling loved, my darling. But you hurt me by sharing our secrets with that deceitful man," Benjamin said in a way to promote a feeling of sympathy.

Cindy, somewhat indignant, responded, "You never once cared about my pleasure. For you, it was always get on me, and get it over with."

Demetri was aware that his lack of understanding of human sexuality was not helping right now!

"Alex may not have made love, but he understands women better than you ever will," Cindy continued.

Demetri was becoming impatient, and it showed as Ben responded to Cindy in a fashion that was a little too familiar, and *Ben-like*.

"Oh, now I see. You fancy this Alex, don't you? Well, my little meth whore, you will never know his love, or the passion from his loins! He retains those desires for another. The nurse who brings you the drugs that don't make you feel like I can, that is who will get his love, not you!"

Cindy began to sob at the hateful and painful words that Ben laid upon her. Demetri rejoiced and knew he was back in the game. He had struck the chord he could play to bring down this man of Gabriel's God.

"Ask him during your walk tomorrow. Then you will know I don't lie to you, and I will be your *love* forever! Only me, and then you will trust me, and do what I say." Benjamin proclaimed.

The night watch Deputy that relieved Johnson looked up from her tablet and shook her head at the mumbling and crying of her companion. "This girl has real problems," she thought to herself.

Alex decided he would not have traded one minute of the phone call he had with Courtney last night for sleep, but as he listened to his alarm ring this morning, he might sell a kidney for another two hours! Stumbling out of bed he began his morning ritual. He looked at himself in the mirror and caught a glimpse of something he had never seen before. There were very evident dark circles under his eyes.

"Holy Cow, if I don't get some time off, they're going to make me work at the county morgue!"

George Bingham stopped Alex as he scanned his key card to enter the facility to begin his day. "Hey, I have missed you lad. They seem to be working you to a pulp lately. If you need somebody to talk to, I'm your man."

"Oh Georgie, you just miss my coffee! Don't try to sweet talk me," Alex laughed!

George responded, "Truth!"

Entering ward fifteen that morning, Alex moved past room two very stealthily so as to not be noticed. He knew if Cindy were to have seen him, he would have felt obligated to go into her room, and thus most of his day would be occupied by her and his other patients would suffer from lack of attention. He felt terrible that he hadn't paid much attention to Mr. Sinclair lately. "He must think what a poor manservant I have become."

Alex could not help but glance into room two as he hurried by and was surprised to see a new escort sitting in the chair usually occupied by officer Johnson. He knew that this meant his plans to circle back to room two now changed. Entering the room, he realized that Cindy was not in her bed as he witnessed the restraints undone. Alex walked up to the new officer and reached out his hand to her.

"Hi, my name is Alex. I am the day watch attendant here at ward fifteen."

The officer, who seemed noticeably young, returned her hand to shake Alex's and said, "hi Alex. I am Officer Myer. Officer Johnson called out sick today."

Officer Myer was petite, blonde and not nearly as intimidating as officer Johnson. Still, Alex sensed that in a struggle she could hold her own.

Alex replied, "I'm sorry to hear that. I hope she will be okay? Anything serious?"

"Most likely a mental day. No disrespect intended," Myer replied.

"None taken. Is Cindy in the restroom?" Alex inquired.

"Yes sir, she is. She told me that you would be coming for her this morning to take her on your daily walk. She said you were her friend."

Alex replied, "Well, I try to be everybody's friend here on ward fifteen. I am going to make my rounds really quick and then I'll be back to pick you girls up. Not literally, I'm not that strong."

Alex was pleased that officer Myer let out a laugh. He was also glad that Cindy was preoccupied, or he might not have been able to get away to see his other patients.

His neglect of his other patients in ward fifteen had taken their toll as it was almost two hours before Alex made his way back to room two. Cindy was ready to go and sitting in her wheelchair, but she had a perturbed look on her face. Looking as much through him, as directly at him, Cindy spoke, "I was beginning to think you weren't coming for me today."

"I'm sorry to keep you waiting Cindy, but I do have other patients that need my attention."

"I didn't mean to make you angry with me. It's just that I had some important stuff to talk to you about, and you are the only person I feel, you know, that I can talk to," Cindy said in an apologetic fashion.

Alex began to feel sorry that he was a little short with her and motioned to Officer Myer and Cindy that it was a beautiful day outside, so perhaps they should just move on with their walk. Cindy agreed and was eager to start their daily ritual. Her eagerness was partly because she felt something for Alex, and wanted to tell him, and mostly because she wanted to prove Ben wrong.

Chapter 33:
Moment of Deception

CINDY WAS NERVOUS. Despite feeling comfortable around Alex, she sensed Ben did not like him very much. She wondered if Ben was jealous of Alex based on the things he had whispered to her, in her head. Not wanting to be in a wheelchair when she started the conversation with Alex, she asked if she could stand up and walk. Officer Myer agreed and with Alex comfortable with Cindy taking his arm to steady her, they walked.

"Alex, once again I'm sorry to have been so short with you earlier. I look forward to our walks, and I wouldn't want you to stop taking me out into the sunshine. I honestly don't know why I have not desired to be out in the sun lately. I guess it has something to do with you," Cindy told Alex in a tender way.

Alex wasn't quite sure how to respond to Cindy as he wanted her to feel comfortable with him, but he didn't want her to be getting the wrong idea about his attention.

"I'm glad you enjoy our walks. Making you feel comfortable and open to express your feelings is what I do," Alex responded as a customer service agent would speak to an inbound caller. He realized that was not the best of responses he could provide her, as she could misinterpret what he said.

"I wanted to tell you that you remind me of my Father. He is a pastor, as I mentioned. Are you a believer in Jesus?"

Demetri was not at all pleased with the way this conversation was heading. It was not his plan to listen about this human's belief in Gabriel's God. He must find a way to distract Cindy and move her away from this and back to his control. He began by having Ben speak in Cindy's head.

"This is not your concern, my love. His beliefs have nothing to do with how he feels about you. You mean nothing to him other than a paycheck. He cares for his nurse only. Ask him.........ask him!" Ben pleaded.

Alex could sense that Cindy was suddenly distracted, but not in a pleasant way. He knew it was forbidden for him to discuss his personal religious beliefs, but he also knew that Cindy's primary hope at having a good life here on earth, was if she could either be connected or reunited with Jesus. He pondered just exactly how to answer her, and he was somewhat grateful she was distracted so he could mull it over in his mind. He decided the best avenue was to skim along her question and try not to be too specific.

"How was it being raised as a pastor's kid?" Alex asked Cindy. "I hear that sometimes, it can be tough," he added

Cindy was no longer distracted by Ben, and her focus and attention had returned to Alex. She asked, "Do you think I'm pretty?"

Alex was a bit thrown by her newest question. How she departed from asking about his belief in Jesus, to wanting to know if she thought he believed her to be pretty, Alex glanced at officer Myer with one of those, *"what am I supposed to say,"* looks. Before he was forced to give Cindy an answer to her questions, she spoke, "My parents always told me I was beautiful, but growing up in a church where your dad is the pastor, boys were afraid of me. If we had a dance, or youth outing with the church, and a boy began to pay even an inkling of interest in me, my mother would send me home or away from the venue."

She went on to explain that she received a letter from her parents, and they wrote to her that the man who attends to you here at the hospital, the man who was talking to you when we came to visit, impressed them. They hoped that he was able to spend as much time as possible with me. They just sensed he had special qualities.

"You're the first boy my parents....my Mother.... didn't send me away from," said Cindy like she was confessing to a priest.

"I guess that's why I asked you if you believed in Jesus. I wonder if when I get healthy, am I pretty enough for you. If you are a believer, then my parents will allow me to see you!"

Alex was lost. He was treading on ground that he frankly did not know how to manage. Having fun with Andrea Best was one thing, but he sensed this girl was way more fragile, and he could cause her damage.

"Cindy, first let me say that I think you are very pretty. Any man would certainly agree with me. I would be proud to be your friend, but I hope you can understand that this hospital, my bosses, forbid me from ever being romantically involved with a patient I cared for," Alex answered her question with all the kindness he could offer.

He witnessed a small tear beginning to fall from her left alabaster eye.

"Are you devoted to another woman?" Cindy quizzed.

"I'm not going to lie to you, yes, I have another woman that I care for very much."

Ben, with a cynical voice into Cindy's head interceded, "See, I am the *only* one who has ever loved you.

You belong to me silly girl. Now you shall listen to me and do everything I say!"

Cindy turned to officer Myer and requested that she and Mr. Dante return to her room. As Alex sat her in the wheelchair, he was disturbed to notice her gaze seemed far off. Like she was not present on this earth. Perhaps it was because she had been crying, but for a moment Alex thought he saw her alabaster eyes turn red!

Chapter 34:
The Dream

EXHAUSTED, ALEX DANTE PUSHED THE CAR ALARM on his keychain and trudged into his modest home. He opened the door and turned on the table lamp in his living room and plopped onto the lumpy old couch. The events of the day with Cindy Firestone had followed and troubled him the entire day. He decided that tomorrow he would sit down with George and share the events. George might be much older than he, but with that age came a lot of wisdom.

He knew he was too tired to prepare anything to eat, so on his way home he sacrificed flavor and health, for a greasy hamburger, fries, and a chocolate shake. Since Alex did not drink liquor often, he figured this was the next best thing to drown his sorrows. Unwrapping the fast food, he took a big bite of the burger and saw the grease had squirted out onto his powder blue scrubs. It was too late, and he was too tired to care. The difficult part is, he wasn't sure if he had a clean pair of scrubs for work in the morning. By the time he had consumed his makeshift supper, Alex stumbled like a drunk man into his bed, and the bastion of paradise offered by his comforter.

Switching off the light on the nightstand next to his bed, he was sure he would be asleep before his head hit the pillow, and he was.

Alex fell into a dream state very quickly. Alex often remembered his dreams because they were very vivid. The dream that night was no different. Alex dreamed he was at the hospital. He sensed it was at the start of his shift, as he was just entering ward fifteen, except this didn't look much like ward fifteen, it was an odd mix of the dining and visiting room at the hospital. The lights were dim, and he sensed it was dark outside, which was not the time-of-day Alex worked. It seemed like he could barely move through the hallway, and he wasn't exactly sure what he was supposed to be doing?

Alex struggled to move down the hallway when he noticed a figure that he didn't recognize. The figure appeared to be elevated off the ground, but he wasn't sure how or why? As Alex moved closer to this figure his eyesight strained to see just who the figure was. In his dream he came to recognize the figure was Cindy Firestone.

Cindy was standing on a wooden chair. She was in powder blue medical scrubs, just like his. Her hands were stretched out in front of her, and he was straining to get to her because she had a perfectly tied rope in the form of a noose around her neck. What was odd about her standing on the chair with the noose around her neck is the rope dangled to the ground. It was not attached to anything in the ceiling, and there was nothing above her to attach the rope to, even if she could.

Alex moved closer to Cindy and heard her cries.

"Please, please, help me. Please, please!"

Then she jumped from the chair with it falling beside her to the floor. Somehow Cindy hung with the rope around her neck, but it was not connected to anything. But it was taught resulting in strangulation. Grabbing her around her

Kevin Wollenweber

waist, but despite being a strong and capable man, he couldn't steady her enough to provide any slack in the rope.

Alex jolted awake with her gurgling cries for help, still echoing in his ears.

"It must have been the double cheeseburger," Alex grasped for an incoherent answer, as he fell back to his pillow.

Chapter 35:
No More

IT HAD BEEN A WHILE SINCE DEMETRI FELT CONFIDENCE. He felt powerful and in command. The results of the day had yielded exactly what he wanted, and that was for Cindy to return to him fully. He decided that the events of this possession had been his greatest challenge so far, and the time had come to gamble her soul, and his peace, no more. This girl intrigued him, perhaps more than the woman from 1920, but he was not inclined to risk any more time just for the sake of his infatuation. What must be done, must be done!

He formed his persona of Benjamin Tasker and stood before Cindy as she slept. Gently shaking her left shoulder, she woke to see him standing there.

"I mock you not, my love," Benjamin gently spoke.

Cindy was embarrassed to look at him and tilted her head away from the side of the bed to which he was standing.

"Truth is sometimes painful. I won't belittle you with *I told you so*," He added.

"I want you to take my pain away. Like you have always done," Cindy cried in surrender.

Ben's hand went to Cindy's hair as he replied to her request. "Yes, it is time for you to be with me. Not in this world, but in a place, we can be happy and at peace, together."

"How?" Cindy inquired.

"Follow exactly what I tell you to do. I will distract our police escort so she will need to leave your room. Tell her you need to use the restroom as she is leaving and ask her to remove the restraints. Laugh, and make her believe you will be fine to go to the restroom by yourself. Joke with her and tell her not to worry, you won't try and hurt yourself. When she leaves your room, go into the restroom, and look on the shelf over the toilet. There is a roll of gauze on that shelf that your nurse, yes that same nurse who will not allow you to have Alex, uses to change your bandages on your beautiful leg. You will take that gauze and wrap it around a bar on the window in your restroom." "With that same gauze you will wrap it around your neck several times until you feel it is tight enough to choke you. Once it is tight enough to begin to choke you, lean forward, away from the window. Soon after, you will be free, and with me," Ben assured her with full righteousness.

Cindy looked puzzled by what Ben had just said.

"But then I will choke to death. I will be dead. This type of death is a sin. Are you dead, Pipeline?"

"Death is only a passing on to a better place. A place without pain. A place with me, and you, and a god who deserves you. Not the God of your father," Ben answered to reassure her. "Also, how fitting that the method and the material you use to join me came from the harlot that Alex desires," Ben laughed!

The pain of her life was too intense at this moment to ignore his words. Dead or not, Ben was all she had, or would ever have.

The plan was set into motion and although it took more manipulating and time than Demetri had planned, Cindy's police escort complied with everything she asked and left the room. In a trance, Cindy walked into the restroom with only Demetri posing as Ben, to encourage her. She managed to take the gauze and wrap it several times around a metal bar in the restroom window. There was just enough gauze in the roll to wrap it around her neck very tightly and she began to cough.

As Cindy felt it beginning to become difficult to breathe, she glanced up towards the window that held the gauze tightly around the bar. She still marveled at the beauty of the sunrise casting its light on the day.

Demetri was not pleased with the day. Darkness and the night hid things. This was much more to his liking, but he could wait no longer. Soon he would be praised by his master, and Heaven's Host would be defeated once again by his cleverness.

Cindy stood with her back and heels touching the wall and simply leaned forward to begin her journey towards Ben. She felt pain and discomfort, but Ben reassured her it was only temporary. He promised, soon her pain would be gone, forever.

Chapter 36:
Cindy's Journey

THE SUN WOULD SHINE TODAY and unfortunately that would mean he would have to take Cindy on her courtyard walk. If there was ever a day Alex had prayed for rain, it was today. He pulled into the hospital employee parking lot and for the first time since he started working there, Alex felt anxiety. He could not understand why, except he just had a feeling that today would be an interesting day. Maybe good, but perhaps bad.

The dream he had last night still troubled him, and as he walked into ward fifteen, he had a sense of relief as everything seemed normal. There was no Cindy standing on a wooden chair, reaching out to him for help as she prepared to do herself in. Alex let out a small sigh and walked to the breakroom at the end of the corridor to stow his belongings. He couldn't wait for George to join him today, and he could use the extra strong coffee he brewed.

Something caught his eye as he glanced towards the door to room two. The door was completely shut. Alex couldn't recall when that had ever happened since Cindy arrived. Peeking into the window with the wire mesh, he also thought it odd he couldn't see Cindy lying in her bed or sitting in her wheelchair. His sense of responsibility kicked in and he felt compelled to enter the room. He would use the excuse he was checking to see if officer Johnson had recovered from her illness and returned to her post as Cindy's escort.

Cautiously he pushed the door open and slowly entered to discover that either Cindy, or an attending officer were there. He also thought it odd that in the corner of the room sat Cindy's wheelchair. Alex noticed the door to the restroom was slightly cracked so he stood outside the door so as to not intrude on any privacy, and called out in a soft voice, "Cindy.... Officer Johnson.... anybody....are you in there?"

Alex received no response, so he called out the same inquiry in a little louder voice. For a moment he thought about getting on his radio and calling for a female attendant to come to ward fifteen to assist, but he realized that might cause some panic around the hospital for no reason.

"She probably had an early morning visit with the doctor, and they forgot to notify me, or put it on her schedule," Alex reasoned with himself.

"Okay ladies, it's Alex, I'm coming in to check on you so better let me know now if you don't want me to open this door," Alex called out as he gingerly opened the restroom door and peeked in.

Alex used every bit of training and instinct he had with what he witnessed. Grabbing his radio, he called out for staff to come urgent to ward fifteen, room two, for a possible suicide. Her knees were buckled beneath her, and her skin color was a pasty blue. After calling out for help, Alex ran to the suicide locker, he extracted a cutting tool to sever the gauze that was serving as the makeshift rope she had used to fashion and wrap around her neck. He lifted Cindy up with one arm and cut the gauze with his other. She slipped limp from his arms and onto the floor.

He rolled Cindy onto her back and checked her for vitals. There were none. He removed the gauze from around her neck and then Alex began to perform CPR. He continued chest compressions and mouth to mouth until other attendants and nurses began flowing into room two and the restroom that held Cindy's lifeless body. Alex relinquished CPR duties to his other associates, but took his turn in succession whenever he could squeeze in. The feeling that this was his fault engulfed his thinking. Not giving up trying to save this girls life had become even more important to him, as he recalled his dream.

The surreal elements of that dream, and the reality he now faced were too much to handle. He wouldn't give up, and those around him tried to encourage Alex to take a rest. They didn't want to face a second casualty knowing that Alex was becoming exhausted. It wasn't until the Emergency Medical Technicians showed up with the advanced equipment, that Alex began to back away. He felt a hand gently touch his shoulder and looking up he saw Courtney. In her gentle and sympathetic eyes Alex could understand he must back away and leave the outcome to the EMT's and medical staff, and God.

Closing his eyes for a moment he continued to hold Courtney's hand that she had placed on his shoulder. Alex prayed. He prayed that God would intervene and allow this girl to live. He prayed that if it were God's will to save her, he would complete the work he had started in her and bring her to a decision to follow Jesus.

Demetri was excited and relished in the thought that soon his master would arrive to take delivery. His work would be admired among his master's faithful, and he would be allowed to relax at his beloved lake and sit on the dock he felt was his earthly home once again. He gazed in amusement as the humans hooked up machines that sought to show signs of human life from her lifeless body and injected her with fluids that would prove fruitless. This truly was one of his finest works, he admired.

Alex stood and looked at the EKG machine as it made no recognition of life or hope of prayers answered. A doctor had entered the area where Cindy laid on the floor, and began to discuss with the people surrounding the young girl, with the once beautiful alabaster eyes, that calling the time of death was inevitable. Just as the doctor spoke, "I'm going to call it," the EMT that was preparing to shut off the EKG machine and begin the process of un-hooking the probes that connected to Cindy's body called out, "We have activity. We have a rhythm!"

Chapter 37:
The Meeting

ACTIVITY INCREASED AT THE ANNOUNCEMENT that Cindy had regained a pulse. However slight it was, she was fighting to return to this earth, and this life. With every passing minute those signs of life became stronger. The doctor quizzed the group attending to Cindy who had initiated life saving techniques on this patient. Alex raised his hand ever so slowly.

"Well done. Probably saved this girl's life." praised the doctor.

The praise Alex received from the doctor was nice, but it didn't begin to console how upset, but at the same time relieved, Alex was. The ambulance crew placed Cindy on a gurney and rolled her out of room two towards the waiting ambulance that would carry her to Mariners General Hospital. His administrators gathered around Alex to request if he was feeling up to sitting down with them to discuss the events that led up to the discovery of Cindy in the restroom.

Alex agreed but asked if he could just have a few minutes to gather himself. The bosses all decided that was in the best interest of everybody and offered Alex all the time he needed. He told them he would meet them in the administration conference room in an hour, and everybody left ward fifteen except Courtney and Alex.

"You gonna be okay, Alex?" Courtney quizzed sympathetically.

Alex seemed distracted during Courtney's inquisition and apologized for not acknowledging her question. She repeated herself, "Will you be alright?"

Alex smiled as he now focused on Courtney and replied, "Sure, I'll be fine. Thanks for being here for me."

Alex seemed to brush himself off like he had just run through a dust storm and began to look around room two. "I have to leave everything where it is for the investigators, so until they are finished, I am just going to lock up Cindy's room and check on the rest of the ward. Then I will go meet with the brass," Alex offered like he really was just talking to himself.

Courtney gently grabbed Alex's arm and spoke softly, "okay then, I'm going to go back to my rounds, but if you need anything, call for me on the radio."

"Will do," Alex affirmed.

Courtney touched Alex on the cheek and departed ward fifteen to continue her duties. Alex sat in the red padded chair that usually held the attending Officer which for some reason was empty during Cindy's attempt to depart from this earth. He bowed his head and thanked God for this miracle. He prayed for her recovery and turned what transpired tonight over to God to serve his purpose for her, and also Alex's life.

Just as Alex raised his head from communion with his God, he was startled by man standing in the room with him. He was a large man of exceptional build, and hair that was so blonde it glistened off his brown skin like strands of illuminated gold. Alex was always proud of his own physique, but this guy put him to shame. He did not recognize him as an employee of the hospital, and he wasn't dressed to represent the EMT's.

Alex stood to address the stranger. "I'm sorry sir, I thought the room was empty except for me. Can I help you with anything?"

There was a gap of silence that made Alex question if the man could understand English because he certainly had heard Alex's question. The tall and muscular man glanced around the room that once held Cindy Firestone. His glances harbored amusement at the surroundings until his gaze became focused on Alex speaking to him.

"Sir, can I help you with anything? I need to close off this room unless you need something?" Alex inquired. The man smiled at Alex which was a gesture that would not normally make him uncomfortable, but today, and this smile did.

The man replied towards Alex in a voice that seemed familiar. "Can you see me?"

"Sure, I can see you. You're here aren't you," Alex half laughed but felt uncomfortable at the same time.

The man discontinued the obnoxious smile as he continued to nonchalantly walk around room two. He answered Alex's question, "I am here. I am confused as to why you can see me unless I wished it to be so. I did not wish for it!"

"Well, sorry I see you sir," Alex said apologetically. It became clear to him that this man must be a patient, and somehow snuck in during all the chaos. "If you will just let me know your name, I can help you get back to your room."

"This is my room. Well, at least it was my room. It was my room when I was with the woman," The figure replied.

Alex seemed perplexed by the man's statement. Nobody but staff and the police knew that there was a woman in room two, and he knew nobody could know her by name. "What woman?" Alex questioned.

The man answered, "The woman Firestone. You call her Cindy. Her name is Cynthia. She was mine. Mine to keep and mine to give!"

This boast from this stranger made the hair on Alex's neck stand up. He thought for a moment to try and excuse himself with a reason that would not alert this man and start freaking him out. He didn't want to spook this guy because somebody needed to find out how and why this *freak* knew so much about Cindy! Alex decided that it was best to use his training and skill to make this guy at ease. Even though Alex was well built himself, this guy could more than likely hurt him fairly easily.

"So, my friend, if you would like to sit down, please feel free to use this chair," Alex offered as he pointed to the chair he was using. "Can I ask you your name and how you know Cindy? She will want to know you came to see her and I can get word to her you were here," Alex explained as he tried to converse with the stranger.

"Demetri is the name I am called," He answered.

"Do you have a last name, Demetri?"

"I am not of your world. I am not flesh and blood like you. Therefore, I cannot understand how you can look upon me?" Demetri replied.

Alex was even more confused by the path their conversation was heading, and he was becoming ever more conscious he was way out of his league of abilities with this person.

"Ah, so, uhm, tell me, are you an alien from another planet?" Alex carefully asked in an earnest manner.

Demetri seemed a bit perturbed by this conversation. "Do not patronize me mortal from Gabriel's God. I am a created being who serves my master. My presence here is supernatural. I am a guardian to the woman. I am here to deliver her to my master. In that purpose, I have apparently failed," Demetri said with a look of despair.

"So, you are an angel?" Alex quizzed.

Demetri laughed loudly and boisterously at Alex's question. It amused him like he had not been amused in many years.

"Few of your kind call me by that name. They reserve that pleasantry for the Host of Gabriel," Demetri answered in an almost condescending tone.

Alex stared at the figure before him, and a few silent moments passed between them. There was something unusual about this man. Alex could not quite place his finger on it, but his instinct halfway believed what Demetri was telling him.

"I understand," Alex answered as he nodded, "so then you are a demon!"

Chapter 38:
Redemption

CINDY SLEPT AND DREAMED. Her recent dreams had been haunted by the appearance of Ben Tasker, but in this dream, he was gone. The only man who existed in her dreams today, was her father. He came often because she was perpetually asleep. She couldn't wake up because she didn't know how. Cindy felt that was a fair trade. To stay asleep, and see Ben no longer, and visit with her dad.

Cindy recognized these appearances of her father, Glen, as being dreams. She knew she was sleeping but she did not care. Even if he wasn't real, and only a dream, it seemed real enough to her. Today was no different. She looked to the left of her hospital bed in this dream, and there stood Glen Firestone. He grasped her hand and kissed the top of it as tears fell from his eyes.

Glen confessed, "I am so sorry baby! Mom and I are so sorry we caused this to happen in your life. We will do anything to make you better. We love you; Jesus loves you, and we will pray every day for you."

Cindy smiled at her dad's tenderness. Even though this was a dream, this is exactly what her dad would say. She knew her mom and dad loved her but were always pushing her towards Jesus, which in-turn only caused her to draw farther away from them, and away from humanity into this abyss she now occupied.

"Daddy, I love you and mommy too," she cried. Wiping her tears from her eyes she looked at her father and continued in all the honesty of her soul. "I don't believe Jesus wants me anymore. He cannot want me. Nobody wants me."

In that moment of confiding to her father she felt hopeless feelings for life eternal. Cindy felt a touch on her other arm opposite of Glen. Cindy could not look over to her right. It was impossible for her head to turn that direction. It was much like wanting to run in a dream, but you just cannot. All she could look upon was the hand that was resting on her right arm. She witnessed the forearm draped in the sleeve of a stark white robe. The robe was as bright as she had ever seen. It appeared to glow. She couldn't gaze any further up than that. She wanted to see the face that belonged to this hand, but she just wasn't able. The hand rested gently and gave her great comfort to be resting on her arm.

Cindy glanced back at her father to see his head bowed. She felt joy and peace for the first time in an exceedingly long time. This is when she heard a voice speak to her. It wasn't in an audible tone or even English, but she understood it. She understood what it said very clearly.

"I will not leave you or forsake you, my child. You are precious to me. I have known you before you were in your mother's womb. Come unto me and I will protect you, and comfort you, and you shall dwell with me forever."

Looking back to the hand that rested on her arm, Cindy noticed an intrusion into the wrist. It pierced completely through to the other side. She believed the promise of the voice but wasn't sure how to come to it.

As she turned back to get understanding of what had just happened a light pierced her eyes. It was blinding and the sting hurt. Cindy struggled to contain the brightness and gain focus of why this light had come upon her. Did it have something to do with the voice she just heard? She struggled to gain focus on her surroundings when it became clear to Cindy what was occurring.

Her father was gone. The hand that rested on her arm was gone. She was awake in the real world.

Chapter 39:
Formal Greeting

THE DEMON HOLLERED WITH DELIGHT at Alex's revelation. "There you go, boy! Now you have finally joined the rest of your kind in understanding what I am. Or so, what you call me. I am Demetri the Demon," Demetri cackled with a slight sense of spite in his voice.

Alex was stunned by this interchange he was having with Demetri and was more encouraged to just leave this man as quickly as he could and let the security team deal with him. It bothered him to know that this intruder could mess up room two, but he also knew he would be scolded for not reacting in a safe manner and removing himself from the area and danger. Alex knew he had a clear path to the door but getting out of ward fifteen could be a challenge. He was fast, but the main door to ward fifteen did not open or close in a quick fashion, and this person could easily catch up to him.

Demetri calmed down and spoke to Alex in a like manner. "I sense you doubt my explanation as to who, and what I am. Don't you, boy?"

Alex responded, "Well, if you believe you are a demon, Demetri, then who am I to question you. I would appreciate you not calling me a boy since we appear to be close to the same age."

Demetri chuckled at Alex's statement. "First, let me explain that the word *Demon* is not accurate. I am an Angel! I am as much an Angel as Gabriel. I simply follow the true god of this earth. I am his servant. Secondly, I am over three thousand years old! To me, you are a child," Demetri spoke in a defiant manner.

"Okay, if you are an Angel, Demetri, then you have supernatural powers. You can leave this room and reappear at will. Show me you have these powers, and I will question your origins no more," Alex challenged.

With that challenge to Demetri, Alex watched his companion suddenly disappear. Alex stood dumbfounded. Demetri reappeared as quickly as he had left and stood before Alex. His long flowing golden braid down the center of his back was gone. His head was bald and shining.

"Do you prefer my head to be hairless, or as before I left you?" Demetri asked like a love-struck schoolgirl.

Alex found it impossible to answer Demetri's question. He was in shock, and his senses could find no argument to suspect that Demetri was anything other than what he said he was.

"Okay, I believe you, Demetri. What do you want here and with me? I do not follow Satan. I belong to the *other* side."

Demetri responded, but as he began, Alex noticed a small tear that had formed and begun to flow from Demetri's eye, and down his bronze cheek. Demetri felt it too, and seemed a bit distracted by the appearance of this tear.

"I am not here for you. I have no power over you because Gabriel's God protects you. I was here and together with the girl with the light eyes. It was my duty, to my master, to deliver her soul to him. You have no right to call him by name, no right!" Demetri bellowed. "I have lost! In my existence I have never been denied in my duty! I need to know how and why she survived! This was to be her time to depart this earthly life, but it is not too late. She is still mine. Her mortal life was not yours to spare. You have no power over me, or should you see, and speak to me!"

Alex had no experience to relate the obvious torment, confusion, and denial this demon was having.

For the first time since encountering Demetri, Alex understood he could see these creatures, but why? He felt emboldened by what Demetri said. He did have power over this demon. He was protected by his faith in Jesus, and this was a special gift provided by the true and living God. Just as Demetri was a servant to his master, Alex was a servant to Jesus.

"Demetri, you are correct in understanding one thing. You have no power over me. You have no power because I am a child of the true and living God, who is Jesus Christ. It was Jesus that defeated you! Not Cindy, not me, just Jesus. One day you and your master will come to declare that fact and every knee shall bow, every tongue confess, that Jesus Christ is Lord," Alex spoke without fear as a summer evangelist.

With those words Demetri was suddenly gone, and Alex was left alone in room two, of ward fifteen. He turned to walk towards the entrance door to ward fifteen and glanced back towards where Demetri had once stood. He was hoping that Demetri would reappear so he could send one last parting comment his way, but he was no longer there.

"Oh, by the way demon, if I have anything to say about it, Cindy will no longer be yours! I believe her choice is still in play!" Alex said defiantly to nobody there! Alex turned to exit ward fifteen and went to his meeting.

Chapter 40:
Awake

GEORGE CAUGHT UP WITH ALEX as he strode very quickly to his meeting with the administrators.

"Hey kid, slow down, I'm an old man," George called out to Alex.

"Sorry George, I'm in a hurry. I'm late to the debriefing of the suicide attempt," Alex responded.

George, realizing how tired and pale Alex appeared, grabbed him by both arms and looked him in the eyes and spoke looking directly at Alex, "you look frazzled, Alex. Don't be afraid to cut the administrators short and go home. You can use the rest, and they will keep you here despite it's their job to look after the welfare of people! "By the way, incredible job you did today. I am proud of you, kid."

Looking as if he was in disbelief of George's praise, he answered, "You have no idea what was involved today."

"Perhaps you should try me some time," George smiled and released Alex so he could hurry to his meeting.

Alex stopped and called back to George, "Hey Georgie, can you monitor the *room* cameras in ward fifteen. My replacement was running a little late, so the ward currently has no attendant. Also, if you notice anybody that does not belong there, can you come pull me out of the meeting?"

George acknowledged Alex's request. Just outside the meeting room where Alex prepared to meet with his superiors, he slid to the floor and rested his back against the gloss white painted cinder block wall. He leaned his head back against the wall and closed his eyes. His mind raced with everything he had just witnessed. Despite the heroic reaction he displayed in saving Cindy Firestone, those memories paled in comparison to his meeting with Demetri. He couldn't help but feel confused, bewildered, and exhausted by that meeting. What did it all have to do with him, he wondered?

Three miles away from the Astoria Mental Hospital, Alex and Ben, Cindy Firestone was becoming more alert, and focus was returning to her senses. She realized this was not her room at the Mental Hospital, but this was a hospital room. A nurse smiled at her as she took her blood pressure.

"Where am I?" Cindy asked.

The nurse explained that she was at Astoria Mariners Hospital and incredibly lucky to be alive. Cindy noticed the presence of yet another Policewoman in attendance. The nurse continued to let Cindy know the doctor would be in to see her shortly. Her throat felt very sore, and it seemed like every muscle in her body ached. A doctor arrived at Cindy's bedside and asked her if she remembered trying to hang herself in her bathroom at the other hospital?

Cindy couldn't recall trying to kill herself, but it certainly explained why her throat was hurting so bad. She thought for a moment wondering why she had wanted to die. The failure to complete the task didn't cause her to feel discouraged or pain at still being alive. In addition to the pain in her throat she felt an even more intense pain in her chest and abdomen.

"Doctor, why does my chest hurt like somebody stomped on it? It's hard to breathe," Cindy inquired.

The doctor finished the poking and prodding of her examination of Cindy, and in a matter-of-fact way answered her question, "your attendant at the Mental Hospital broke your sternum and a few ribs doing CPR. It happens. He did a valiant job saving your life!"

Cindy was not surprised that it was Alex who saved her. She hoped she would get to see him again. Despite being in more pain than when she withdrew from drugs, she wanted to thank him for saving her. The doctor continued to explain to Cindy that she would be in intensive care for a few more days, and if she needed anything, to let the nurse know. As the doctor left her room, she thought for a moment she must be sleeping again, for it was during her sleep, and dreaming, that her father appeared.

Standing next to her bedside was not only her dad but her mom. This time she knew they were real because she almost passed out from the pain caused by her heart beating in her chest.

No eyes were dry during this reunion. Glen and Margaret were gentle, knowing the extent of Cindy's injuries. They pulled up chairs next to Cindy's bedside and held her hand like they would never let go. Just like in her dreams, except this was real and her mother was also there. They were reunited and together.

She noticed a woman standing behind her parents at the doorway to the room. Her police escort and the woman seemed to know each other and were talking to each other. Glen and Margaret made no reference to what had transpired recently with Cindy, and only talked of the joy their daughter brought to them. After several minutes of rejoicing about their reunion and sharing *fond* memories of each other, Glen's mood turned a bit somber.

"Cindy, baby, this lady Officer behind us is Pamela Harris. She is an Investigator with the St. Helens Police. She has been helping mom and me with your case. I know you must think she is on the side that is out to get you, but she truly has been there to try and help us, and you," Glen spoke softly and carefully.

"How about Ben? I mean Pipeline, have they caught him yet? Did they know he has been seeing me in the hospital?" Cindy quizzed.

Glen, Margaret, and Pam looked at each other with that look of concern and confusion. Glen was unsure just how to answer her question.

"Cindy, we will discuss…uhm…Ben later. This is about you," Glen answered. "Investigator Harris allowed us to come see you today to let you know you won't be going to trial for your involvement with Ben Tasker. Your doctors at the other hospital have decided you need to spend some time with them, and that would be better than going to trial."

"So, I will be back with Alex to watch over me?" Cindy eagerly asked.

Once again, all three looked at each other with a sense of confusion until Margaret spoke up. "I believe Alex is the young man that was her attendant at the hospital. The one we sensed was *different* and Cindy responded to him so well."

"Yes, that is Alex," Cindy agreed.

Glen and Margaret offered they would do all they could to make sure that Alex was once again, her attendant.

"Then I'm glad to be going back to that place. I have so many things to ask Alex. Not about love or romance or anything like that. He is in love with a nurse. I need to ask him about my dreams," Cindy confessed.

Glen and Margaret were pleased that Cindy accepted the truth after they tried to candy coat that fact a judge had determined that Cindy was unfit to stand trial due to insanity. The District Attorney had decided not to pursue charges based on the judge's ruling and that Cindy would be placed to be a ward of the state, until determined to be mentally competent to return to society. Based on the recent past, Glen and Margaret knew their daughter needed much help. They wished it could be different, and that their daughter had led a normal and healthy life, but at least she was alive, and they could visit her often. Glen wanted to ask Cindy about her dreams, but his instinct told him not to do that today.

Chapter 41:
The Visitor

DRIVING HOME, ALEX COULD FEEL WINTER coming on. On the coast of Oregon, winter was different, he imagined, than anywhere else. It wasn't unusual for the rain to freeze, and to get cold enough to occasionally provide a dusting of snow. He had often wished it would just dump eighteen inches of the white powder, covering everything, and causing the coast of Oregon to just shut down. The snow would be like a blanket of borax. Cleaning everything and stopping everybody, even him.

He was tired beyond comprehension, but he knew that his experience with Demetri would not allow sleep to come easily. Just the understanding that demons truly existed and prayed upon souls that had not decided for Christ, was disturbing. He considered if he could see Demetri, he could also see Angels.

He exited his car and took in a full breath of the cold mist into his lungs. Closing his eyes, he also felt that same mist on his face. It felt remarkably good, and if he had not started to feel chilled, he might have stood out in this weather longer and gazed at the Columbia River dumping its frozen supply into the Pacific Ocean.

Alex gazed at the ground where he first saw the needle that contained some junkie's momentary bliss. He thought it would be remiss of him to not recognize that what was contained in that syringe, was resourced by a demon. Perhaps even Demetri himself. He stopped to wonder if, and when, he would see Demetri again, or any other demon as matter of fact. It wasn't pleasant to entertain them, and he was still trying to navigate this ability that God endowed him with.

Opening the door to his meager coastal home, he placed the empty thermos into his sink and decided he would wash it later. He needed to relax. The events of the day would have exhausted anybody even without his encounter with Demetri. Flipping on the lamp by his lumpy sofa, Alex was startled. Sitting on the torn and tattered chair across from his sofa, the chair used for the occasional, rare guest, sat Demetri.

Alex gained his composure after being startled by his presence and scolded Demetri. "Hey, I don't know how you so-called *angels* work where you come from, but we humans don't just pop into somebody's home uninvited!"

Demetri pulled at the torn fabric of the chair that he was sitting on as if he were amused by it. "My apologies to you as master of this dwelling. I have sat in many human's dwellings, but none of them had the ability to see me like you. My mistake for forgetting this, but I have many questions for you," Demetri said, as he continued to stroke the fabric of the chair like a pet kitten.

"Well, unlike you, I assume, humans need to sleep, and I am very tired. I don't intend to go to sleep with a demon hanging around in my living room watching television," Alex replied in a sarcastic tone.

Alex noticed that Demetri's long golden braid had been restored.

"You look less like a demon with hair," Alex commented.

Demetri grabbed the end of his braid and looked at it and returned his focus to Alex with a slight smile.

"Human compliment. My first," Demetri chuckled.

"What questions do you have, Demetri? I can answer the quick ones and then it is my hope you will be gone just like earlier today," Alex asked. "Before we proceed, I will also teach you human hospitality and offer you some refreshment. Do you eat, or drink? Would you like some coffee? Perhaps a glass of water, I understand it is hot and dry where you come from," Alex asked without a hint of disrespect.

"I do not eat or drink, this is not ordained for me. One of my questions for you is, do you see others of my kind? Those who serve the master of the earth and also those who serve Gabriel's God?" Demetri asked in an earnest and inquisitive way.

Alex was perplexed on just how to answer Demetri. He did not feel it was in his best interest to divulge information to this being that thrived on deception, and who used information for evil, and torment. He thought back on the man he had seen in the cafeteria at the hospital. The tall slender man in the black leather jacket that Andrea had advised to him, was a demon.

He thought it safe to answer Demetri's question as long as he did not divulge too much information. "Yes, I can see others like you."

Demetri stroked his chin as Alex supplied that answer. "Okay, a last question, and I will leave you as you have requested of me. My question is, you said to me that you did not beat me. Your God beat me. How did he beat me?" He asked.

Alex simply answered, "Because I asked him. I asked him for Cindy's sake."

"But Cindy is mine. It is too late for her so why would your God do that for her?" Demetri seemed puzzled.

Alex responded, "Because my God is Jesus Christ, and he loves her. As long as she breathes, the same as I do, she still has a choice. Your power is not as significant as you might believe!"

With that retort Alex found his tattered chair empty. Alex fell to his knees and prayed that he was not worthy to wage this battle with a fallen angel. But if God desired it of him, he would continue to be a witness for the demon. A witness for just how great his Lord is. His final prayer request to God was for protection and the peace of sleep.

Alex slept that night, as the Host of Angels watched over him and brought him slumber.

Chapter 42:
Cornerstone

A COUPLE OF WEEKS HAD PASSED since the events of Cindy's attempted suicide. Alex had not received a visit from Demetri since his visit at his home, and he would be dishonest to say he missed him. Alex wondered how Cindy Firestone was doing, and if she was recovering to the point that she had any brain function. More so, he wondered if Demetri had returned to his catch. He had not accepted his defeat during their last visit, and he doubted that he had given up.

All that Alex could hope for is that God saved her for a reason and would protect her should Demetri attempt to take a second shot at her soul. He prayed for Cindy every day. His rounds were uneventful, and he began once more to enjoy his patients on ward fifteen. Mr. Sinclair had forgiven him for being absent and not attending to his needs as his manservant. Alex had to admit he enjoyed this role as Sinclair's butler.

Courtney had made her normal rounds, and they discussed that everything seemed to have settled down enough so they could arrange their schedules to go on that first evasive date. Alex was ready and excited. Since Demetri had departed and there had been no sign of whatever it was in the black leather jacket, he felt more secure he wouldn't encounter one of his demons in front of her and had to explain.

Alex sat in the breakroom of ward fifteen enjoying his morning jolt of caffeine, when George arrived to join him.

"Top of the morning to you chap," Alex pretended to tip his hat to George. It was apparent that Alex had just been with Mr. Sinclair.

"Hey kid. You hear the news," George said as he extended his dirty cup towards Alex's thermos. "Your girl is coming back," George offered.

"My girl?" Alex pressed.

"The Firestone girl. This time she will not be a criminal though. She has been made a ward of the State, so she will be coming to a ward near you," George laughed.

Alex didn't quite know how to feel about this news. Obviously, she needed to be under observation as a suicide watch, but it also meant she was functioning and coherent. The mentally challenged were never placed in ward fifteen. It also meant her police escort would no longer be needed. If she was a ward of the State, it meant that she was diagnosed as mentally ill. He knew it would be futile to explain that Cindy's mental illness, her schizophrenia, had to do entirely with demon possession.

"Sure, I'll just take that piece of information to the administration," Alex thought like a stand-up comedian delivering a rebuttal to a joke.

What worried Alex the most is would be getting Cindy Firestone back, also means Demetri comes with her? The thought made him shutter. Just that same afternoon Alex was alerted to the arrival of his return patient. She was assigned to room four which used to belong to Andrea Best. Alex thought it a fitting gesture that is where she was being assigned and would be her residence for a long time to come.

Kevin Wollenweber

With all the apprehension he had about Cindy's return, he was also tempted to discuss Demetri with her. She might not be able to comprehend the role he played in her life, and potential attempted death, but he must try and discuss it with her. Otherwise, he sensed he would not be doing the work to which he was anointed.

Cindy arrived with little fanfare. She was reeled into her room in a wheelchair, and she was able to exit the chair with very little assistance and climb into her bed. Alex placed what personal items she was allowed in the built-in dresser along the wall. He turned towards her and greeted her in his usual fashion, "Welcome back Cindy. Glad to see you again. The red button attached to your bed is if you need me for anything and the green button is to turn your television on and off. Unfortunately, you will need to signal for me if you need to change the channel."

Cindy smiled a big smile, and despite all that she had been through Alex could see she was looking much better, and her alabaster eyes seemed so much clearer. She pointed towards the television and said "At least I have a TV this time. This room is much better than my last."

Alex chuckled and noticed she was wearing a nasal cannula attached to oxygen. He began to disconnect the apparatus from the portable machine and hook it to the larger one in her room.

"I'm on oxygen. Apparently, the big brute who worked here broke my ribs when he saved my life," she giggled as she spoke.

"Well, what a creep. We will make sure he doesn't come anywhere near you," Alex pretended to be stern.

Alex completed his set up in room four of ward fifteen. He made his notes on her chart noting he had covered all the housekeeping check points and told Cindy he would be back to check on her.

"Alex, how about our walks? Do we still get to do our walks?" Cindy asked with anticipated trepidation.

"Cindy, it's too wet and cold to walk outside, but I will sit and talk with you here in your room, as often as I can. If it's exercise you are after, you will just have to ask physical therapy to get you down to the gym, and get you on the treadmill," Alex laughed, as he walked away from her room.

Cindy smiled at his comment. It was his company she desired the most, and she anticipated his return.

Sitting down at his desk to catch up on paperwork is something of a luxury Alex rarely gets. He booted up his computer and decided that today was the day he would finally get caught up on patient logs, and notes. He grabbed his written notes, turned to his first patient, and pulled up their chart. Just as he was about to begin, the phone rang. The last thing that Alex expected is for the phone to ring, as it was rare for him to get a call. Especially an outside call.

He answered the phone, "Hello, this is Alex Dante, ward fifteen attendant, how can I help you?"

On the other end of the phone was Glen Firestone. He responded to Alex's greeting in the same professional manner, "Hi Mr. Dante, I'm not sure you remember me, but my name is Glen Firestone. Actually, we have never officially met. I am Cindy Firestone's father.

"Of course, I remember you Pastor," Alex responded.

Glen was once again surprised that the staff at this hospital knew he was a pastor. He continued, "I'm sorry to bother you while you're working, but I know that Cindy arrived back at your hospital, and her mother and I would be remiss if we didn't call you to say, thank you! Cindy speaks very highly of you, and this brings much comfort to us that you are there with her."

Alex was grateful that he had this opportunity to speak to Glen. He felt a bit selfish in what he was about to ask, but he felt God was leading him.

"Pastor, I don't mean to pry into your relationship with Cindy, and what I am going to ask you has no demand for a response, but are you and Mrs. Firestone going to come and visit Cindy here at the hospital anytime soon?" Alex inquired.

"Funny that you ask me this question Alex. We are coming to visit Cindy tomorrow at three. Why do you ask?" Glen inquired.

"Sir, I wanted to talk to you about something. Something that involves Cindy, but what I need to talk to you about violates every policy we have here at the hospital, and I would need to speak to you in private. Off the record, if you get my meaning," Alex was cautious as he proceeded.

There was a pause in Glen's response. It was obvious that Alex had dropped a vague bombshell.

"Mind giving me a little background, son. Is what you're asking is to meet with you first before we meet with Cindy?" Glen replied.

"Exactly, sir. I need to ask you some questions that are *faith* related, and the topic is delicate. Actually, I need to discuss something with you that I am not comfortable even going to my own pastor. Shoot, it's a risk even going to you, sir. You might think I should be a patient here," Alex treaded lightly.

"Are you a believer in Jesus Christ as Lord and Savior, Alex?" Glen inquired.

"With all my heart and my soul pastor. When I tell you what I need to tell you, well, I'm not sure what you are going to think," Alex responded.

Glen and Alex decided they would meet at one o'clock at a café down the street from the hospital. Glen asked if it was okay with Alex if Margaret joined them. He was fine with her attending. Glen and Alex hung up with each other and Glen sat and stared at his phone. What had started as a simple call of grace, and thanks, had now turned into a great mystery. Glen had no clue that the very foundation of his beliefs, and cornerstone of his preaching, were about to be turned upside down.

Chapter 43:
Choice

THE TV CHANNEL PLAYED SOME GAME SHOW that Cindy couldn't quite figure out. She didn't really care as she waited patiently for Alex to return to her room. Glancing up at the window with the brown painted bars that showed the paint peeling from years of changing temperature and wetness, she gazed at the condensation as it formed a picture frame around the window.

She could still feel the touch of the hand she knew was Jesus on her arm. She was excited to share her dream with Alex knowing he would not condemn her or declare her even more insane than she already was. She needed to know exactly what it meant, and as much as she loved her father, she did not believe he was the person to interpret her dream. She trusted Alex to think it out thoughtfully, and carefully.

He needed to come soon or she felt as though she would bust. Guts and all would come spilling out, and Alex would have to arrive to once again, save the day. The one thing Cindy did not want to happen today was for Ben to come. But come, he did. His legs were folded in a nonchalant fashion and his arms across his lap. Ben sat grinning at her and saying nothing.

Cindy was uncomfortable with him being there and thought for a moment to hit her buzzer and have Alex come and remove him from her room. She knew Ben thought he was tough, but he would be no match for Alex. After a few moments of uncomfortable silence Ben finally spoke, "Hello my love. Nice to see you again. Sorry I didn't come visit you in your other hospital, but I got tied up with some problems."

"What, tied up with gauze around your neck like me," Cindy said with no emotion.

"Touché," Ben offered up with reconciliation.

"Regardless, your attendant thwarted our plans to be together. Now look at you, back at this place and in pain just like before."

Cindy closed her eyes in an effort to see if it would make Ben go away, but when she opened them, he was still there.

"It hurts me to not have you with me Cindy. I have a *new* plan that I have devised, that should do the trick. As always, I just need you to follow my lead," Ben explained to evoke her sympathy.

"I don't want to die to be with you. I do not even want to be with you while I am alive. Please just leave me and get out of my head," Cindy impatiently urged.

"Where is this coming from? After all I have done for you, and this is how you thank me? What, do you believe Alex will somehow leave his woman for you? A skinny, ugly girl like you," Ben spewed with total spite.

"No Ben. I don't think Alex will be with me. It is against the rules here at the hospital, and Alex obeys those rules because he is a man of God! Yes, God!

It was hard for Demetri to sit and hear this blaspheme without getting angry.

Do you believe in God, Ben? I mean the God of the Bible. The Father, Son and Holy Spirit? Do you believe and follow them, Ben?" Cindy asked with defiance.

Had Cindy known this type of conversation would accomplish the goal she originally sought, she would have done it a long time ago, for Ben no longer sat in the chair next to her bed. He was gone, and Alex Dante knocked on the door to her room.

She was delighted to see his face and welcomed him into her room. Cindy invited Alex to sit in the chair that only a few seconds ago contained Ben Tasker. They began their discussion with the schedule that Cindy was going to be following. She listened intently as Alex reviewed the times, and days she would be seeing the therapist, counselor, and going to group sessions. As much as she knew Alex was intent on being a professional, she found her mind wandering with the desire to discuss her dreams, and what they might mean.

After affirming that she understood what Alex had just reviewed with her, he asked her if everything was okay and was she settling in. Cindy did not have any patience left and had to tactfully dive into her questions.

"While I was in the other hospital, I had a dream every time I slept. My father was in it and stood at my bedside on my left. He seemed as real as he could be. On my right I could feel a hand gently touch my arm, but all I could see was a hand, arm, and part of a bright white robe. The hand had a hole pierced through it. I could see nothing else. Alex, I need to know, was that Jesus? He spoke to me and said he loves me. *Me*! Could that have been Jesus?" Cindy implored like a child waiting for Christmas morning.

Alex listened intently to the story of Cindy's dream. He explained to her that dreams were often a gift from God to reveal something he wants us to know. He continued to explain to her that he wasn't an expert in dream interpretation, but he knew that what the voice said is absolutely true.

"Jesus does still love you! He wants you to follow him," Alex said in earnest!

Then Cindy, unable to contain herself, blurted out, "I see and talk to Ben Tasker. He was just here before you came in. He sat in the chair you are sitting in now. He is the one who told me how to kill myself in the bathroom, and he wants me to follow him now!"

Every fiber of Alex's training would have made him call for a doctor since she was threatening suicide again. He decided he wouldn't make that call this time. It was all noticeably clear to him now. Ben Tasker was dead, but he was being used, or at least his image and voice were, by Demetri. It sickened his stomach to discover what he already knew; Demetri was not going to give her up.

"Cindy, you must listen to me, and I ask you to believe me. What I am about to tell you is not from Alex Dante, the attendant in ward fifteen. Not Alex *your* attendant. It is from Alex, your friend, who wants you to live. And live a life for Christ! Ben Tasker is dead. You are not talking to the dead corpse or the ghost of your boyfriend. You are possessed by a fallen angel, a demon, by the name of Demetri! Ben Tasker *is* Demetri, and he wants your soul for Satan. His mission, his desire is to deliver souls for Satan! You *are* his mission, and he wants to deliver your immortal soul! Do you understand what I just told you?" Alex called out with a frantic sense of urgency,

As soon as Alex revealed what he knew was true to Cindy, he felt as if he had just done the wrong thing. This girl was still in the clutches of a powerful demon, and who knows what Demetri could be capable of?

He hoped it would provoke Demetri to manifest himself. He wasn't afraid of Demetri or his power. Alex believed he knew why he could see demons now. This was a battle that he, Alex Dante, had been chosen to fight. Fight for those souls. Demetri was afraid of him! He had never faced a human with his power before. A human with the power of Gabriel's God!

Cindy began to cry. She knew Alex spoke the truth, but she was afraid. What if Jesus was through with her? What if this demon Demetri had already won? How could she be rid of him and his image of Ben Tasker, even if she wanted to? Alex sensed that Cindy was experiencing a moment of inner turmoil. He took this defiance against the powers of evil, knowing that he was placing his job in jeopardy by what he did next, but he just had to trust in the Lord.

He grabbed Cindy by the hand and bowed his head and prayed. "Lord, I submit your child Cindy to you. I believe that she believes in you, but she is held captive by the true deceiver. Lord, I command that he release her heart. Give her the strength to confess that you, and you alone, are her God! Let her acknowledge that you died on the cross, rose from the dead for her, so she can have everlasting life with you. Give her this strength, in Jesus's name, amen."

Lifting his head after praying, Alex caught a glimpse of Cindy with a blank deathly stare looking around him to the figure standing behind him. He did not feel the need to even turn around because he immediately knew standing in their presence was the demon Demetri.

In all his mortal manifestation of tall, bronze magnificence, long golden hair flowing down his back, Demetri spoke, "Let me introduce myself to you Cindy. Yes, you have come to know my presence as Ben Tasker, but I took that form so as to not frighten you. Unlike your friend, Alex here, who frightens you with a God that died and now wants you to follow him, I, unlike Alex's God, and my god are, and always have been alive!"

Cindy was amazed at the physique and size of Demetri. He was daunting in stature with his long golden hair. Despite his size, Cindy found an inner strength to speak to him.

"You may have not wanted to scare me but taking the form of a dead Ben Tasker was deceitful. What do they call you since you are obviously not Ben?" Cindy questioned him.

Alex turned to face him and said, "He is the demon Demetri."

"Ah, your dear friend here tries to deceive you again. He is enamored with that word *demon*. I am as much an Angel as the Host of Heaven," Demetri proclaimed.

"Why then can Alex see you? You have no part of him?" Cindy asked.

"This is true, and unfortunately I do not know why, or how he can look upon me. I suspect it is because his God allows it, to deceive people as to my power to grant them peace without pain," Demetri explained.

Alex had grown tired of Demetri's attempts to win Cindy to follow him in the path to Satan. He turned from Demetri to discontinue their confrontation and he looked directly at Cindy and spoke with all the confidence he could show her, "Cindy, I think I know why your father appeared in your dreams."

Cindy's attention was so directed towards Alex at this time that he was convinced Demetri could have started to dance a jig, and it would not have distracted her.

"I believe your father was the one that first introduced you to Jesus. Through his preaching and being the man of God, he planted the seed of who Jesus is. He is a friend to your father and loves him, and your dad loves Jesus. Your father loves you as much as he loves Jesus, and he wants you to surrender to Christ. His asking brought Jesus because he loves you that much. The reason you couldn't see the face of God is because he is Spirit. I believe your father brought God to your bedside so he could let you know he was still there for you! All you need to do is choose. The time to choose has come," Alex finished his evocation.

Demetri clapped in a sarcastic manner at Alex's explanation. "All your father and his God have done for you is to cause pain! I, and my god, offer you relief from that pain. Your choice is evident and clear."

The tears flowed steadily from Cindy's beautiful eyes. Her sobs masked the evidence of why her head was bowed and either Alex or Demetri knew that at the moment, Cindy was indeed making her choice.

Chapter 44:
The Alarm

COURTNEY SAT AT THE NURSE'S STATION making her chart notes and was finding it hard to concentrate. She had Alex on her mind. She was concerned for all he had been through over the last few months, and now that Cindy Firestone had returned to ward fifteen, she could tell just how preoccupied he was. Something was troubling him, but they were so new in their relationship that she didn't want to pry into his life. Not yet anyway.

She was patient to wait for whatever hurdles Alex had to jump over. He was a kind, and sweet soul, and although she had gathered a lot of attention from many men, Courtney sensed that Alex was the right guy for her. They really had not had much opportunity to begin dating, and starting to get to know each other, but why that might be important to some girls, it wasn't to her. She believed in destiny when it came to matters of the heart and Alex was her destiny.

It became evident to her that she might need to be the one to push Alex a little. As handsome as he might be, he was also a little shy. Courtney had provided more than enough leads that she wanted to pursue this relationship, but he was so easily distracted, and she also wasn't sure if he always picked up on her hints. She decided that since things were steadier and tamer around the hospital, and his ward, even since the return of Cindy Firestone, she would stop by ward fifteen a little early before administering medications and try to nail down a date for them. It could not hurt to take the lead, she thought.

With having the satisfaction that taking the lead was the thing to do, Courtney returned to making her log entries. An alarm went off which startled her, but not as much as the radio call that followed shortly after.

Please have security respond to ward fifteen, room four.

Courtney's heart skipped a beat, and then the worry set in.

Chapter 45:
Angry

WHEN CINDY RAISED HER HEAD, Alex knew she had made her choice for Christ! Demetri knew her decision had not gone in his favor and began tossing the contents of Cindy's room against walls and towards the door that led to the hallway.

Alex covered Cindy as she crouched in her bed to protect her. Hitting the alarm button next to Cindy, he hoped that the arrival of security to her room might result in Demetri's disappearance then, and maybe forever. As majestic as Demetri might have been, and as appealing as he made himself to those humans he wished to exploit for their souls, this Demetri was not attractive at all.

Cindy was frightened by the actions of Demetri, but when she prayed for Jesus to enter her life, she felt it. Unlike when Demetri must have entered her for the first time, Cindy felt this. It was as if a blanket of warm fleece on a snowy day had covered her. Whatever Demetri, who was posing as Ben Tasker might have promised her, this feeling was different. For the first time since she could remember, she felt peace and no pain in her mind or soul. No drug could ever come close to this feeling.

Alex wasn't quite sure what would happen when security showed up. Would they see a hairbrush and toothpaste flying around the room without a method to cause it? He wasn't quite sure how he would explain to his superiors why *stuff* was being tossed mysteriously about the room. What he did know for sure, is before him and Cindy, was a demon that had been defeated, and he was angry.

Demetri's anger resulted in the expansion of his frame almost like an Olympic bodybuilder. Alex could only imagine why those that opposed the Vikings were terrified of them in battle. This was one pissed off demon.

"Denounce your God! Denounce the God of Gabriel now," Demetri cried out!

Alex heard the main door to ward fifteen start to open. He knew that any moment now the security team and his friend George would come charging into the room. As difficult as explaining what had transpired here would be, at least the outburst of a three-thousand-year-old creature would be squelched. He continued to cover and protect Cindy until what occurred next perplexed Alex and was beyond his immediate understanding.

George Bingham walked into the room. No security team was ready to bring control and order to the room and the ward, only George, without the appearance of a care in the world.

Chapter 46:
George

GEORGE BINGHAM WAS IN NO WAY AN OPPOSING FIGURE. One might say he appeared old and chubby. At his age, the staff at the hospital all gave George credit for having had a stellar military background, and he was very efficient at checking people in and out of the facility. But to say he was enough muscle when something was going down, would be a stretch.

Alex was shocked and not sure what to do with his friend showing up alone for an emergency-panic call. Demetri had stopped his ranting and tossing items when George entered the room. He moved towards Demetri, hands crossed in front of him and bellowed, "Well, well, what do we have here?"

Demetri seemed disoriented by George's appearance and apparent ability to see him just like Alex. He glared at George to try and get an acknowledgement that this human was indeed witnessing his presence. George helped him reach that conclusion quickly.

"Yes, I can see you much like my friend Alex here," George spurted.

Alex, still crouched over Cindy looked first at George's face, and then over at Demetri, supposed that the look on Demetri's face was very similar to his, and their looks projected the same astonishment.

Demetri called out screaming at George, "I did not reveal myself to you. You should not be looking upon me unless I have decided to let you!"

Demetri was using his defensive posture to the best of his ability, but with another mortal being able to see him without invitation, was quite concerning to him.

"Don't flatter yourself," George scorned Demetri.

Frustrated even more that he was challenged by this unimposing human, Demetri decided he must regroup and resettle. He was unsure that Cindy was not being deceitful, and he would attempt to enter her. Once again, in the blink of an eye, Alex found Demetri was gone. With his supernatural powers of coming and going at will, he could certainly see Demetri when he appeared before him, but Alex did not have the power to know where he might go in retreat.

Shrugging his shoulders at George, Alex spoke with much trepidation in his voice, "I don't know where he went George? I never know where he goes. Is he gone forever, and *wait*, how can you see him? Why did you come to my panic call alone? And how could you see the creature?"

Alex seemed to stumble over his words and questions for George. "Don't worry, Alex. I can see what you see, and always have. Soon I will explain it to you, but for now, I know where he has gone, and I must follow him there. I have called out an all clear in ward fifteen. Nobody else from my security team will be arriving. Please settle this young woman and bring order back to her room," George commanded.

"George, has he returned into Cindy?" Alex inquired.

"He tried, but this is no longer an option for this demon."

With that statement barely out of George's mouth he disappeared before Alex's eyes. He must now exercise every ounce of patience he had until George would return because his questions were vast, based on the activities since George's arrival at ward fifteen.

Alex moved Cindy's feet beneath her blankets and adjusted her pillows under her back and head. He smiled at Cindy to reassure her that she was going to be fine. She gazed back at Alex with her alabaster eyes that seemed much clearer than he believed he had ever witnessed them before. She smiled back at him and spoke with a quiet assuredness.

"Demetri is not with me Alex. I heard you ask if he was with me. He isn't allowed to enter me anymore," Cindy offered in reply.

"God is powerful and good. Praise be to God," Alex exclaimed!

Alex sat in the chair next to Cindy's bed. He was exhausted and nothing he had witnessed would be resolved anytime soon, but now he had to wonder who, and what, was his friend George?

Chapter 47:
The Lake

TO INHABIT THE BODY, MIND AND SOUL of a human host was as natural to Demetri as snapping your fingers. After all, he had done it over one thousand times in his existence. Standing in the room confronting Alex, and the old man who mocked him, was not pleasant for Demetri. When he retreated to inhabit his host Cindy, he did so to regain his power and regroup. Neither of these humans could match his power. He just needed to gather his edge once again.

How dare they challenge him or his master! He was ashamed he had felt defeated and believed this girl had turned to Gabriel's God. He wished to enter into Cindy Firestone and as with every mortal soul before, thought it into existence. For a moment Demetri was disoriented. This time did not seem familiar to him. He did not sleep as mortal's do, but his feeling was one like he experienced while inhabiting a human that had awoken from a slumber. He struggled to gain orientation as to his surroundings and was lost until he heard the water slapping on the pillars of the boat dock.

"Ah, my lake, my *beloved lake*," Demetri thought with newfound relief.

It was only a brief moment later that the realization set into Demetri that he had not intended to retreat to his lake. His lake was a place of tranquility. The only tranquility he could inhabit was in victory, and he was not yet victorious. At this moment he should be dwelling in Cindy.

Flat on his back with his golden braid underneath him, Demetri's head almost touched the very edge of the dock that entered the lake. He knew it was cold outside because frost had formed on a portion of the lake and was frozen. Feeling cold or any temperature change was not something he could experience. He was confused as he watched the light, connected to the dock rafter above, begin to flicker. Between the light beginning to try and emit the glow of its bulb, Demetri began to make out a silhouette of a figure standing at the opposite end of the decaying dock near the pole holding the light. He pushed himself up from the dock, still feeling slightly dazed, and began to recognize that the figure on the other end was the older human who had confronted him in Cindy's room.

Like a man that had begun to pull himself to his feet after getting punched and knocked out, Demetri addressed his dock companion. "I see that not only can you see me without invitation, but you can follow me where I go! I believe the mortal Alex, calls you George. Well George, you have abilities well beyond him to be able to follow me here!"

George moved closer to where Demetri had erected himself. He admired the beauty and physique displayed by this demon. George replied to Demetri, "I can see why you retreat to this place. Its earthly beauty is to my liking also."

"Well, its beauty is reserved for me and me alone. I command you to leave me here. You distract me from my task, and I do not desire to continue to have you here despite your obvious powers," Demetri demanded. "You are not my master! So, leave me now before I allow others of my kind to inhabit your mind and devour you," Demetri waved his hand as if to shoo a fly as he spoke to George.

George laughed so hard and loud that if there had been mortals close by, they might have heard a clap of thunder.

"You are right, demon," George settled enough from his burst of laughter to speak to Demetri. "I am *not* your master! You are deceived, much like all that are like you. But I do know your master very well."

A seagull flew over the two conversing on the dock and called out to them. The gull was winging his way to the coast to feed and bed down on this cold and frosty winter night. It came into Demetri's thoughts that this mortal, just like him, did not seem affected by the cold. He saw no frozen breath as he spoke.

"You are not mortal. I see no breath of mortality. This explains why you can see me and follow me here! Declare who *is* your master creature. Do you follow my master, or do you follow the God of Gabriel?" Demetri challenged George.

A bright and moving light emitted from the heavens. As the light moved from far off it headed fast towards the boat dock. Demetri watched in awe of the sight and was curious as to the source of its power. As it reached the rustic and decaying structure that these two stood upon, it settled directly above George. Demetri was intrigued by what this illumination might have to do with this being that was standing before him.

The light began to engulf George from top to bottom. Demetri wondered if his master had summoned the light to extinguish this foe, devour him, and allow Demetri to continue with his earthly duty of serving him. As much as he appreciated his master doing this *work* for him, he felt no threat in challenging and defeating this creature whether he be like him or follow Gabriel. As the image of George began to be extinguished by the light, Demetri thought that his original intent was to be rejoined with Cindy, and he was being distracted. Why then was he at his lake, and being forced to endure the challenge of this old and inferior creature?

Just then the light ceased and retreated from the being that stood across the dock from him. As the light shined no longer, Demetri fell to his knees.

Chapter 48:
Every Tongue

STANDING BEFORE THE KNEELING DEMETRI, in all splendor and magnificence, was not the portly old man who had previously debated with Demetri. Although many thousands of years had passed, he recognized him as the Angel Gabriel.

"Demetri, I worship the true and living God. I am of the Heavenly Host that sings his praise, and worships the King of Kings, the Lords of Lords. You do not need to call him *my* God! You might as well get used to calling him Jesus Christ, Lord of all," Gabriel proclaimed.

Demetri was speechless and beyond reproach. He knew he was no match for Gabriel. It had been over three thousand years since he had stood before Gabriel, admiring him, wanting to be him!

"Gabriel, I have no words for you. I challenge you not. If you have followed me here to declare that the woman with the alabaster eyes now belongs to your master, then I resend my authority to you," Demetri said as he cowered and continued to kneel.

"I have not followed you here, demon. The woman you have controlled in evil and sin, sent you here."

"I do not understand what you say, Gabriel? The woman had the power to send me here?" Demetri quizzed.

Gabriel offered a broad smile as he answered Demetri, "Yes, she has the power of the Holy Spirit that now dwells within her. She has received the baptism of that spirit, and you can no longer dwell or inhabit her."

Demetri had come to realize that *his* lake was no longer a reward. What was once a place for him to have peace, to love mortality, despite his hatred for mortals, would now be exposed as a place of pain and suffering for him.

Gabriel moved to the side of the boat dock and sat. His heavenly robes were hiked up to his knees and Demetri watched with amazement as Gabriel plunged his Angel feet into the water. His feet were not contained in the water for long, as he quickly removed them, he immolated a shiver to show how cold the water was. Reaching down with one hand, Gabriel used it to scoop the water from the lake, bringing it to his mouth, and drink it.

Demetri watched and yearned. Even though Gabriel, like him, was not mortal, his God allowed Gabriel to experience the pleasures of mortality.

"Witness the quenching of my thirst, Demetri. Just as I take this liquid into my mouth and taste its cold, Jesus gives those that follow him, the *living water* of eternal life. His servant Alex Dante has drunk that living water and delivers it to those who are oppressed to come to the well by their own means. Cindy Firestone was one of those who could not come to the well. Many were there to provide that path for her," Gabriel preached.

Demetri had to acknowledge what he had just heard. He had lost. The mortality that he so desired, but tried to deny, had been kept from him by his master.

He felt a burning in his temple as he watched Gabriel rise from the edge of the boat dock. This was a burning that Demetri had never experienced. With the burning he also felt a pain in his demon soul that doubled him over on the very dock he used to revel in his own accomplishment and vanity.

The last thing Demetri saw before jumping into the lake to escape the torment was George Bingham walking away from the dock and disappearing from his view.

Chapter 49:
First Date

ALEX SAT WITH CINDY FOR THE REST OF THE AFTERNOON. He left to occasionally check on other patients in ward fifteen, but Alex believed he needed to be present with her, just in case Demetri, or more importantly, George returned. Alex had so much confusion about what his future held. What all of this meant, and where he fit into everything. He had to trust God more than ever.

When his shift was over and his replacement had come to relieve him, Cindy was asleep. He hated to leave her, but he needed to go to somebody that he could confide in. Someone who cared for him, and hopefully would not run from him as if he were stark raving mad. He told the attendant who came in his relief that he had nothing to pass along, and to please keep an eye on Cindy as she had a rough day.

Alex knew that was nowhere close to the complete truth, but it would have been futile to try and explain the events of his day. As he grabbed his belongings, walked out of ward fifteen, and immediately sought out what he hoped was his bastion of relief, Courtney Blair. Fortunately, he found her finishing up her rounds and preparing to depart. Her face turned from tired and solemn, to relieved and beaming, when she saw Alex. Coming to each other in a very long embrace that neither wanted to end, they eventually broke from each other.

"I was so worried about you," she said as she lightly placed her left hand on Alex's face.

"I am so blessed to have you thinking about me," Alex replied.

He continued to offer her only vague explanations to the events of his day and the emergency radio call that had caused her to worry. Alex made a plea for Courtney to accompany him to grab a bite to eat so he could talk with her in private. Concerned and very curious to hear what Alex had to tell her, she heartily agreed to join him. They agreed to drive separate to a local café near the downtown area of Astoria. Alex watched carefully to make sure Courtney didn't lose her way, and they parked in the small parking lot of Paxton's Café.

Exiting their vehicles, Alex walked over to Courtney's car and opened her car door for her. She was taken by surprise by his act, since she couldn't recall the last time a man displayed being a gentleman to her. Grabbing her hand, they began their stroll toward the café door. Courtney had a panicked thought that Alex might have asked her to join him tonight to discuss the possibility he didn't want to continue with their young relationship. With his actions since arriving here at Paxton's, she knew those thoughts were unfounded.

She sensed he was distressed by the events of the day and the reason he wanted her company tonight is because he *needed* her. Had Alex been able to read her mind, he would have validated her conclusion as being true. They entered the front of the café and the young woman acting as hostess directed the twosome to a booth near the back of the room. Normally, Alex might have asked for a table closer to where everybody was eating, but this booth would serve to provide the privacy he needed.

He felt compelled to tell her about his recent companion, Demetri, but that was a strange tale that might cause her to end their friendship, let alone what others that might overhear his tale might think! He was concerned about how she would accept his story, but he knew he had to tell her the events that occurred after George arrived. If she believed him crazy, and suffering a nervous breakdown, it could risk everything he wanted in his life, and that was to have Courtney in it.

Alex decided to break into his strange tale with a humorous note. "Hey Court, do you realize this is our first official date!"

She chuckled at his declaration and replied, "And you bring me to Paxton's! If I knew you were such a big spender, I would have sought you out sooner!"

Alex returned her chuckle but in the back of his thoughts he was pleased that she said she would have *sought* him out. This girl was everything he could ever wish for, and for her to say that about him, warmed his heart. They each ordered dinner and once it was delivered, they sat alone in their section of the café and the conversation turned more serious. Alex started from the beginning. Telling Courtney about his first experience in seeing demons and how his encounter was confirmed by Andrea Best. He studied her face as he told her about Demetri. Her look was not one of skepticism as one might suspect. She listened to him intently as he described Demetri and how he had followed him to his house.

Courtney displayed a frightened look when Alex relayed that part of his story. He explained that she hadn't heard anything yet. He finished with the event that happened today and how George had arrived, alone, and could also see Demetri. He told her about how George confronted Demetri and then just disappeared.

"What do you make of George?" Courtney inquired.

"I can't make anything of it. I am worried about my friend, but he didn't seem worried as he spoke to Demetri. George appeared to be in control," Alex replied.

Alex was curious why she didn't seem to question his sanity throughout this entire conversation. Courtney seemed understanding, concerned and like she was totally believing everything Alex was telling her. He felt compelled to ask her.

"So, do you believe me? Do you believe everything I just told you?"

Courtney stared at Alex with sympathetic eyes as she responded. "Alex, I have no reason to not believe you. You are an honest and giving person. I don't understand *why* God chose you to fight demons, but I believe He chose the right person."

They smiled at each other, and Courtney came to the side of the booth where Alex sat and draped her arm around him as if to say, "I trust you."

Alex leaned in and kissed her, and she reciprocated. They sat at Paxton's until closing time discussing their concern about George. Both hoped he was all right and said a prayer to God for his protection. Alex's fears about Courtney thinking he was ill and running for her life were gone. She followed Alex to his house, and they fell asleep holding each other. Neither pressed to be intimate. As believers, they both desired their first time to be in marriage. Just to lay next to each other brought peace and comfort to a troubled Alex.

He slept well for the first time in quite a while.

Chapter 50:
The Protector

ALEX DRANK HIS COFFEE AND STARED at the most beautiful thing he had ever seen. If he could have looked upon her all day, lying there sleeping, he would have chosen that over anything. He longed for the day he might watch her sleep as his bride. He doubted there was another woman who could hold a candle to this girl. Her eyes began to crack open as she caught Alex staring at her.

"Like what you see?" Courtney stretched as she spoke.

"I apologize, who are you again?" Alex laughed in reply.

Courtney threw a pillow at Alex and jolted from the lumpy couch, moved towards Alex, and kissed him.

"Oh, now I remember who you are," Alex said with a hint of sarcasm.

The workday for the couple was just on the horizon and both began to get themselves ready for the challenges that faced them at the hospital.

"I hope that George is at the front door today holding his stained coffee cup. I need to talk to him," Alex sighed.

"Yes, I think he holds some answers to your questions," Courtney answered.

Alex explained to her that he was confronted with another challenge today and that was to meet Cindy's parents before their visit. Courtney could see a perplexed look on his face. He relayed that Cindy's father was a pastor, and he hoped that he could understand the battle his daughter raged with Demetri.

"I have to believe he would be somebody that would understand how courageous his daughter has been. I also must believe that Cindy will begin to recover. She obviously has suffered much, but now, she no longer carries that affliction that was Demetri," Alex offered.

Courtney gave Alex a big hug and proclaimed, "You are the person God has anointed to expose this spiritual battle to those who would believe, and understand, what you have to say."

Alex and Courtney closed the door behind them and climbed in their respective cars and drove down the road from Alex's house. Alex pondered how he would start the conversation with Glen Firestone. Maybe Glen did not follow the same belief in the supernatural existence of demons. Unlike Courtney, he and his wife would think that Alex was as sick as the people he cared for at the hospital.

His anxiety was high, and he still had to do his job until noon, when he would meet with the Firestones. Regardless, he would tell Cindy that he was going to see her parents before their visit. She deserved to know that he was going to divulge her struggle, and triumph over Demetri, and most importantly her belief in Jesus. Courtney must have been in a hurry to get to the hospital because Alex was trailing behind her car, and she had advanced out of his sight.

He just couldn't propel himself to go any faster knowing that this day offered so many challenges that he would need all the help the Lord could provide him. Alex glanced out his driver side window at the mouth of the

Columbia River moving along in its journey to the Pacific Ocean in all its splendor. As his focus came back to the roadway Alex was momentarily shocked to see George Bingham sitting by his side, in the passenger's seat!

At first, he was elated to see his friend George was apparently well, but then the realization set in that George had appeared out of nowhere.

"Sorry to startle you Alex," George nonchalantly said.

"Startle me! You simply scared me to death, George! Where have you been? I have been worried sick about you," Alex expressed to George with a feeling of anxiety.

Pulling his car over to the side of the roadway Alex stopped and put his car into park and turned directly to address his friend. George could feel the tension and anxiety from Alex. He began to listen to George although he wished that Courtney hadn't drove ahead at the speed she was traveling. She needed to see this, or she couldn't see that George had appeared in Alex's car? Regardless, he knew she would believe his retelling of this story when he met up with her.

George began, "Alex, I will ask you to listen to everything I have to confess to you as my time is short, you have been blessed with a power and a gift that you will use to continue to serve our Lord. You have wondered if your ability to see demons and speak to them was the extent of your abilities."

"Yes, I was curious why I only see demons. I am confused why I don't also see Angels," Alex questioned his friend?

George laughed at Alex's question. A light illuminated around George that was so bright that for a moment Alex had to shield his eyes. Once the light began to dim Alex was amazed to be miraculously standing on a boat dock, looking out over a pristine lake. He was standing next to the most beautiful creature he had ever witnessed. Demetri had been impressive to view, but this creature was magnificent.

The creature spoke, "You have seen Angels! I am The Angel Gabriel. I took on the form of George to protect you and to keep watch over you. God has anointed you to be a witness, Alex. Our hospital is a bastion of activity for the agents of Lucifer, but you have the love, and patience to defend those souls so they can be claimed by Jesus. Demetri is a powerful demon, and I was with you knowing he was coming. Our Lord knows everything that will occur as he knew us before we were created."

"Gabriel, will I encounter Demetri again?" Alex asked.

Gabriel continued to explain to Alex that this very lake was where Demetri would retreat for *reward* from Lucifer. This is the one place that Demetri knew the escape from torment. It had now become a lake of torment for him. "It has not been revealed to me if you will encounter Demetri again. Since he came to you out of curiosity of your power and he was defeated, he will be afraid of you. You carried a witness that he could not understand and thus, could not defeat," Gabriel pronounced.

"So, this is where Cindy, with the power of the Holy Spirit *banished* Demetri," Alex asked?

"Exactly. Therefore, you shall be our Lord's *witness for the demons.* You have a wisdom that is rare, and you are *my* soldier from this moment on," Gabriel commanded.

Alex found himself sitting back in his car alone. Gabriel had left him, but he sensed this might not be the last time he would see him. Overwhelmed with the task that Gabriel had laid before him he was also humbled to know he would not be alone. Putting his car into drive Alex pulled out into the street and admired the sun shining through the clouds. Driving into the employee parking area, Alex continued into the building in his normal fashion.

At the front entrance was Jim Hebert, who was one of George's team members. He greeted Alex with a friendly smile. A smile that Alex knew was totally human. He did not stop to inquire about the whereabouts of George that day. He knew that George would no longer be there to greet him every morning. Alex knew it was up to him now. The angel Gabriel had moved on to his other *job*!

Courtney was waiting for Alex as he came to the entrance of ward fifteen.

"Hey, what took you so long?" Courtney quizzed although she didn't give Alex time to answer.

She continued, "Did you see Jim Hebert at the entrance! He said George took a sudden sabbatical. He said he didn't know when George would be back to work. It makes me worried." Courtney wasn't quite sure why Alex was just standing there and smiling at her. The look on his face puzzled her because it displayed a look of I know something you do not.

Then he opened the entrance to ward fifteen and placed his hand on Courtney's back as she pushed her med cart into the ward. In a reassuring voice he spoke to Courtney, "George is fine. I saw him this morning and we spoke. He looked better than I have ever seen him."

Not understanding what Alex had just told her she determined she would just have to trust his calm demeanor. "You are a strange man, Mr. Dante. I trust you will explain more on our second date," Courtney replied.

She continued into Mr. Sinclair's room, but Alex went to Cindy Firestone. He was surprised to see a different woman. She was dressed in newer denim jeans, and she had put on a neutral blouse with a light sweater. Cindy was sitting in the chair that had only recently been occupied by Demetri. A bible was open, and her hand held the page she was turned to and reading.

Alex told Cindy about him going to meet her parents before they came to visit her today. Cindy was grateful that Alex would tell her parents the foundation of the evil abyss that she had been living in, and trusted Alex to deliver the news of her salvation. He patted Cindy on the arm as he started to leave when she abruptly stopped him. He was a bit concerned as to the sudden *grabbing* of his hand by Cindy, but his concerns were quickly put to rest when Cindy opened her other hand and displayed to Alex a simple rosary with a hand carved crucifix on one end.

"Where did you get that rosary, Cindy?" Alex asked with a puzzled look on his face.

Cindy replied, "It came in the mail addressed to me. It was from somebody named Andrea Best who lives in Vancouver, Washington. Look, it had a note with it."

Handing the note to Alex he read the contents. The note read,

"I shall know you throughout eternity. Sisters, who together have defeated the evil one. Holding this item that I give to you, is like holding the hand of the one who created the Angels."

Alex recognized the rosary. It was the rosary that Angela Best had made for her husband.

Chapter 51:
Family

GLEN AND MARGARET FIRESTONE recognized Alex immediately. They shared pleasant greetings and moved into the restaurant and were seated. Small talk and questions about Cindy permeated the conversation at the beginning. Alex realized that the Firestones must be just as uncomfortable with this meeting as he was. Not knowing how to proceed with the uneasy feeling they all were having; Margaret Firestone broke the tension in a most effective way.

Reaching out across the table she grabbed Alex's hands and held them tight. As she held them, she spoke, as she looked him straight in the eyes, "We, I mean Glen and I, have sensed you are *special* from the first time we saw you at the hospital. Our daughter is everything to us, but we have failed her in so many ways. We hope this time at the hospital will be good for her. We pray that you, can validate just how special we believe you are, Mr. Dante."

Alex was overwhelmed with the faith and kindness that Margaret showed. He knew at that moment that the incredible story he was prepared to tell them had a better chance of being accepted by these folks than anybody. He embarked on the story of their daughter's journey with the demon, and through the triumph of salvation and redemption. He explained that the seeds of that salvation were indeed planted by them, so they should know they did not fail.

When Alex had completed his exhortation to Glen and Margaret including detailed recollection of his and Cindy's experience with Demetri, he ended the conversation with, "Well, I suspect you either think me totally insane or you believe your daughter is a changed person through Christ."

Realizing that their meeting time had passed so quickly, they stood to depart for their visit with Cindy. Glen had said extraordinarily little during their meeting, but as they stood to leave, Glen embraced Alex for what seemed like an eternity.

"I envy you Alex. God chose you for a reason. As far as future demons go, kick their butts!"

Cindy was escorted holding onto the arm of Alex into the visitor's dining room. Glen and Margaret had a moment of concern because they wondered who this woman was being escorted by Alex. If it had not been for the beautiful glow of Cindy's alabaster eyes, they might have mistaken this girl for someone else. She had gained weight since the last time they had visited; her hair was curled, and she looked every bit the beauty they always knew her to be.

Alex backed away from the reunion between daughter and her parents. He went over towards the kitchen and watched. Several times during the visit, Alex caught Glen's eyes glancing his way. The look in those eyes showed gratitude. He wondered how long before Cindy's doctors would notice that she no longer displayed the psychosis they had come to see in her.

However long Cindy might need to stay at this hospital, Alex had comfort that Glen and Margaret Firestone held the secret of his gift and power, and he could count on them to keep it. Standing up to stretch and take a stroll around the dining room he strolled over to where the beverage and ice dispenser were. Alex grabbed a plastic glass from the carrier and filled it with ice. Pouring a glass of iced tea, he carried the glass to a secluded table near the rear of the dining room. He thought his separation was in order to give the Firestone's as much privacy as he could offer.

Standing near the back was the figure in the black leather jacket he had witnessed a couple of times before. The figure stared at Alex with a sense of "does he see me?" Alex did not divert his gaze away from the figure. This time there was no mystery. He knew this figure to be a demon and he spoke to him.

"Yes, I can see you, demon," Alex confirmed.

Picking up his ice filled beverage, Alex drank down almost the entire glass and crunched a few ice cubes at the end.

"Who are you to see me, you are a mortal," the figure in the black leather jacket sneered as he clearly envied Alex having the ability to enjoy the beverage.

Finishing the last few gulps of the liquid, Alex stood to face the figure.

"I am Alex Dante. I am a soldier under Gabriel! If you need to know me, you can ask the demon Demetri," Alex professed.

The demon turned his body and face to not look upon Alex and spoke towards the ground. "You defeated the great Demetri. I know of your power. Forgive me, soldier of Gabriel."

"I know not of your business here, but be gone from my sight lest I take the time to vanquish you today," Alex spouted in amazement for the words he chose to chase this pest away

With that declaration, the demon Gayland left the presence of Alex. He marveled that his power to recognize and know these demons was a gift he must harness and hone.

Chapter 52 :
Warrior

SEVERAL WEEKS HAD PASSED since he had exposed his gift to everyone, he believed he could confide in. Glen and Margaret visited Cindy often, and Glen phoned Alex at least once a week to check up on him because he understood how this gift could also be a burden. Having people pray for him would help Alex feel strong. Alex had not seen a demon, or needed to challenge one, since he had encountered Gayland in the dining hall.

Cindy grew stronger every day and immersed herself in the bible. She enjoyed her walks and talks with Alex, and he reveled in how quick she was advancing in her understanding of God's word. They rarely talked about Demetri, which was fine with Alex. The demon no longer posed a threat to Cindy, and the reality of how he had controlled her was understood.

The challenge of being a warrior against the evil supernatural realm was exhilarating, but Alex had not lost sight of his largest challenge which was to conquer Courtney's heart. Second and third dates had come and gone and his affection for her had not diminished. He knew that there had been a promise of a date to The Saturday

Market, and he felt that the right time had come to fulfill that promise.

Alex had arranged for Courtney, and himself, to have a weekend off together, and that she should be prepared for a surprise. He picked her up at her apartment early one Saturday morning. They drove east enjoying each other and all the farm communities and rolling hills they passed along the way. She had waited patiently for Alex to tell her what he knew about George. After Alex shared with her the appearance of George in his car, and that he revealed himself as The Archangel Gabriel, he wasn't sure if Courtney's mouth would ever close again.

"So, you see angels too?" Courtney asked.

"Well, so far, only one, and that was Gabriel," Alex answered.

"I have also seen and talked to George. So technically, I have seen an angel, right?"

Alex smiled and took Courtney's hand in his. "Absolutely you can see Angels. Now that I'm looking at you, this would be number two for me."

She kissed him on his cheek as the city of Portland came into view. Off in the distance to the east the couple viewed the blue and white majesty of Mount Hood. The bridges that outlined the Rose City transported them over the Willamette River and down into the outskirts of the downtown. Alex parked the car within a short walking distance of their destination.

They traveled up the street and began to encounter booths and tents containing hand crafted items, clothes, and smells of wonderful food. Courtney knew he had honored his promise and had brought her to the Portland Saturday Market. After an hour of shopping and eating, Courtney began to laugh.

"What are you laughing at?" Alex inquired.

"I remember what you told me, about every hippy that ever lived, came to Saturday Market to sell their stuff. You were right," Courtney chuckled.

"Well just you wait for what I have to show you next," Alex teased.

He pointed at a booth at the end of a row. On the masthead read the name of the merchant, *Rosary's of The Rose City*.

Standing at the booth with a smile as big as the Columbia River was a familiar face to both. Simultaneously they held out their arms and yelled, "***hippy girl!***"

Chapter 53:
Guest Speaker

WALKING OUT ONTO THE STAGE, in front of what she estimated were at least two thousand people, Cindy looked around at the glory of Seaside Community Church. The clapping had subsided, and she stepped to the pulpit after embracing her father. Composed and confident, she began, "Most of you here today know me, my name is Cindy Firestone, and my father is your pastor. One year ago, I was selling, and addicted to methamphetamine, cocaine and heroin. I left my family and turned my back on Jesus Christ."

After a brief but uncomfortable pause Cindy continued, "I was diagnosed with schizophrenia, bipolar depression, and I attempted to commit suicide. Fortunately, that attempt at suicide wasn't successful. That portion of my story I will come back to later. My story is not unusual. Our mental hospitals today are filled with people just like me. Where my story takes an unusual direction is why I am here today. I am here today to tell you an unbelievable tale. One that you might find it hard to believe me, or even listen to me."

As Cindy addressed the congregation you could have heard a pin drop. She explained the source of her earthly troubles were because a powerful demon had possessed her. Cindy spoke fluently to the crowd in a way that even if you were skeptical about the existence of Angels and demons, she was believable. As she ended her time on stage, Alex, who was her official escort for her speaking engagement, was called on stage to join her. She shared with the congregation how he had been instrumental in saving her life and bringing her to Jesus.

Alex was not expecting to be acknowledged at this event and was a little embarrassed. After Cindy was finished, Pastor Glen thanked Alex for his faith and being part of the miracle that saved his daughter. Cindy's doctors were amazed by her progress and felt that speaking about her addictions and struggles with mental illness, were positive influences in her recovery. Alex was anointed to be her escort when she was allowed to travel outside the hospital walls. She and Alex both knew how, and why, she had recovered. After the event, several people came up to both Cindy and Alex wanting to know more about demons, and how their evil web is spun.

Alex kept his gift to see and talk to Angels and demons alike to himself, and the small group of friends that also knew about his gift, for now. He felt it was best to stay humble and secretive, as it put him in a position to discover more about demons. He did not miss Demetri and was glad there had been no additional encounters with him. The other demons he had discovered lurking about the hospital had become less and less. He felt that they must converse with each other somehow, and they had become aware and alarmed by his abilities. Several had left and not returned.

He wished, occasionally, he had the ability to follow them, and could cage the particularly nasty demons up. Alex wasn't sure what Gabriel would do with them, and he often wondered what had become of Demetri. All he could do with the gift he had now, was to identify who the demon was possessing and try and bring that soul back to God. That would have to be sufficient for now.

Courtney had joined Alex and Cindy at the church. As everybody had left and it was only church staff, the Firestones and Alex and Courtney. They hugged and said their goodbyes, as they prepared to return to Astoria and the hospital. Just as they were ready to depart, a youth pastor at the church came up to Cindy. He asked her what days and times were best to come visit her at the hospital. Cindy assumed that he was just interested in visiting as that is what pastors do, and also wanting to learn more about her story.

Courtney quickly glanced at Alex, who in turn looked at Glen, who smiled and winked at him. Later on, the trip back to the hospital, Courtney filled Cindy in on the reason the youth pastor wanted to come visit her. It took a long time for the redness to leave Cindy's face.

Chapter 54:
Stains

WITH HIS WORKDAY ALMOST COMPLETE, Alex stepped into the breakroom at ward fifteen to grab his belongings. He reflected on just how proud he was of Cindy. The courage she had displayed to get up in front of her father's church and tell a tale that was, frankly, unbelievable as it was amazing! He grabbed his coat and turned to leave when sitting on one of the tables was a stained coffee cup.

Alex immediately recognized it as being George's cup. He smiled and looked around the room as if to find his old friend and Angel might very well have come to enjoy a cup with him. Picking up the cup Alex looked it over with curiosity of how it had arrived there. Realizing his friend was not going to come for a visit he carried the cup to the sink. His first instinct was to pour dish soap in the cup and begin the soaking process to remove the stains that might never come out.

Stopping short of squirting the soap into the cup, Alex picked it up and thought better of exposing it to a cleaning. George would never forgive him for defiling the years of coffee residue etched upon the ceramic interior. He placed the cup back in the cabinet above the sink, laughed and

Kevin Wollenweber

turned off the light as he departed to meet up with the love
of his life.

Chapter 55:
Requiem

THE BARTENDER AT THE OZONE TAVERN on the outskirts of Astoria, looked up at the clock above the bar and decided it was close enough to the last call to announce it to his patrons. With last call, the scraggly young man wearing the Oregon State Beavers ball cap that was positioned backwards on his head, held up his glass that once contained a local distilled bourbon.

The man had just purchased several pull tab lottery tickets, hoping to finally have some luck, which had been so elusive to him recently. The question of whether he should pour the kid another drink entered the bartender's thoughts. He seemed fairly drunk, but he had been a regular at the tavern for quite some time, and he had seen him in worse shape than tonight, so he poured the last call and placed it on the counter in front of him.

After pouring the other few patrons their last drinks of the night, he continued with his duties of cleaning and preparing to close the tavern for the night. After a few minutes, the kid with the bourbon had finished checking his lottery tickets and it was obvious that fortune had not shined upon him with big winnings. The bartender watched as the kid swallowed the last few drops of his last call and held up the empty glass searching for another round.

"Sorry buddy. I couldn't poor you another round even if I wanted to. The register is closed out," The bartender apologetically said.

The kid pulled off his ball cap and began to rub his face with one hand. He needed another drink and ten more after that. His life was crumbling before him. He mumbled to himself, "I'm a failure as a husband, a father, and a human being."

Staring at and taking in the drama that this drunk loser was displaying, the hooded figure that had been sitting next to him, all night as he drank himself to oblivion, made his move. Plotting and confirming that this was the right choice to try again, to get back in the game, he had made his decision.

Demetri entered this kid's mind and soul to prepare it for his master. This time he would not fail, he could not, and he would be restored.

www.ingramcontent.com/pod-product-compliance
Lightning Source LLC
Chambersburg PA
CBHW051509260626
47162CB00008B/2890